Loving I

Cyborg Seduction - Book Nine

By Laurann Dohner

Loving Deviant

by Laurann Dohner

After barely surviving a horrific accident, then being held captive for years by Earth Government, Venice must escape the planet. She thinks she's found the answer to her prayers when she contracts to be a deep-space bride—only to find herself facing an even bigger nightmare. Hiding from her con man "husband" aboard his space station, she comes across an intimidating cyborg...one who could just be her last hope.

Deviant is humiliated when his father suggests he visit a pleasure center to make use of a sex bot. True, the defects he was born with have assured female cyborgs will never consider adding him to a family unit. But he still has his pride. The woman who enters the room, however, is incredibly lifelike, and she quickly has Deviant feeling things he'd never dreamed—right until the moment he finds out she's human. Sort of...

Venice needs Deviant's help to get off the space station. Deviant is lonely, and in need of someone to teach him how to pleasure a female. They strike a bargain, one that has Venice giving up her freedom. But soon it's her heart that's at greater risk. It's easy loving Deviant...even when others are determined to make it difficult.

Dedication

To the love of my life, MrLaurann. You make loving easy every single day of the year. I'd be lost without you.

Cyborg Seduction Series

Loving Deviant

Copyright © August 2016

Editor: Kelli Collins

Cover Art: Dar Albert

ISBN: 978-1-944526-31-3

Chapter One

Darbis Martin is a dead man if I get my hands on that lying, two-faced son of a bitch. Venice crept around the corner, straining to hear any sounds of booted feet. Her fake husband had his men searching for her on the space station, and sadly, they'd find her within a matter of hours. The place wasn't big enough to conceal her for long.

She reached the automated pleasure center and darted inside the door of the reception area. The sex bot inside was a tall thing, had a pretty face, and smiled. "How may I please you?"

"I'm reporting for duty," Venice lied, hiding her stolen weapon behind her skirt. "I'm going into the back and you are to delete any knowledge of my being here."

The pretty bot kept her smile in place. "Of course."

Venice figured it couldn't be that simple but she lunged through the interior door, hoping the thing would actually erase the fact that it had seen her. She was in a world of trouble and her fake husband was the source of it. She should have listened to her sister.

If it sounds too good to be true, it usually is.

She hid behind a large replica bush inside a lounge area for clients of the automated brothel, and tried to think up a plan. First in order would be to get off the station before Darbis found her. Second would be to find a safe place to go after that. Earth wouldn't be on her itinerary.

It had all seemed so simple in the beginning, when Darbis Martin had charmed her during all their vid chats. He'd been funny, intelligent, and handsome. Too bad it hadn't really been *him* talking to her. The ink on their false marriage decree had been dried and dated for over thirty days by the time she'd arrived at Colton Station to meet the real puppeteer.

He had her over a barrel, too, completely trapped. That's when he'd shown her what a devious bastard he truly was by luring her out into space to make her a slave laborer in his private brothel. He invited special visitors to the station he owned, and they wanted real women. Darbis figured she couldn't put up a fight. She had nowhere to go and was stranded on the station.

Her hands clenched around the knife in her hand. She wasn't a whore—and wouldn't become one, either. She'd been desperate enough to marry a stranger, willing to sleep with him, but being passed around to a bunch of men wasn't going to happen. She'd done enough lying on her back, her body being used in another way after the accident that had trapped her in a bed for four years.

Venice moved her legs faster, happy to have some again, and memories surfaced.

She shivered, remembering the vehicle accident on Earth that had disfigured her by taking three of her four limbs and leaving her with no life to speak of. She'd been scarred, crippled, and hidden away in some medical center. She'd become a virtual prisoner, until her sister had found a hacker good enough to discover her location. They'd rescued her and taken her into the underground system.

Darbis had fully taken advantage of her dire situation, and she wondered how many other women he'd sworn to love and cherish, only to force them into sexual slavery to make a profit.

She lifted her chin, knowing she'd gone through too much to end up dying on a distant station, being abused.

The doors to the lounge opened and fear gripped her as two men entered the room. They were both huge, their bodies draped in baggy clothing—but the fact that their faces were covered terrified her more.

Pirates.

She'd seen them walking around the station, the first sign that her new fake groom wasn't a law-abiding citizen, since pirates were banned from all decent stations. Of course it hadn't been shocking, considering he'd married *her*. She'd excused it by wanting to believe Darbis wasn't biased against any living beings. It had even elevated her opinion of him—until they'd met face-to-face.

"It will be fine," the slightly shorter pirate urged in a soft voice. "They are sex bots, programmed not to keep records. That's the positive thing about artificial beings."

The taller one shook his shrouded head. "I don't wish to be here. This is humiliating, Father."

Venice held her breath and watched them through the thick leaves of the artificial plant. They didn't seem to realize they weren't alone, which was perfect for her. The father and son pirates were too distracted by their conversation.

"I know this isn't an ideal situation but you've passed your thirty-fifth year, son. Our females have never considered you for breeding or to join a family unit." The shorter one gripped the slightly bigger, taller man's arm. "You've never had the opportunity to have intercourse."

Whoa! A thirty-five-year-old virgin? Venice winced. She knew most pirates were mutated, had seen footage of their messed-up features on the news, but the son had to look pretty bad for mutant women to refuse to give it up to him. Her gaze darted over him from head to foot. He stood about six and a half feet, the pirate clothes obscuring the skin of his big frame, but he didn't appear misshapen. Just huge. Big-boned and beefy. The poor pirate women were probably afraid he'd crush them or something.

"Father, I don't wish to do this."

"You need to gain experience. Your mother has talked a few of her friends into testing your skills. You will have to really impress them if you want a chance of ever having a family."

"I gave that dream up after I realized I was different."

"I'm sorry." The father's regret sounded in his voice. "I know this is all my fault."

"I'm undesirable. No woman will ever wish to join with me. They don't want to look at or touch my skin. I appreciate Mother trying to entice her associates into testing me but it won't matter. They find me unattractive since I have imperfections that may be genetically passed to any offspring. I truly believe it will be worse if I learn what has been denied me all this time."

"You're a strong male and are important in our society. Most females would enjoy having a male who could elevate their status."

"Be honest, Father. I am realistic about my situation. There are a lot of available males, there is still a shortage of females, and none of them will consider a status upgrade as an equal trade for flawed offspring."

The other man loudly sighed. "Please do this. I don't see you as flawed, and some would feel the same once they got to know you. You might become skilled enough to win over a female. A few of them might consider your unused DNA as a benefit."

"Fine." The taller one didn't hide his anger as his voice deepened into a near snarl. "I'll engage in intercourse with a sex bot. I hope the others don't know about this. I'd never live it down."

"Most of them also visit the automated brothels unless they are joined inside a family unit. There is no shame."

"I bet they had real females first. I'm even disgusted with myself." The tall one reached up and yanked off the material that covered his head and face. "Are you sure it's safe to remove our disguises here?"

Venice knew her eyes widened and her lungs burned for air when the guy turned to glance at the doors of the private rooms. She caught a glimpse of his face and his skin stunned her. He was a dark gray hue, almost a charcoal, and no human could appear that way. He sure wasn't a pirate. His features weren't mutated or covered in radiation sores. He actually was handsome, with strong facial features, full masculine lips, and his eyes were so blue they seemed illusory.

11

His side remained to Venice. Silky, beautiful black hair fell down his really broad shoulders. He dropped the hood-type headgear and unfastened the loose shirt he wore, dropping it to reveal the best torso she'd ever seen. Her mouth fell open at the sight of his thickly muscled arms and sculpted six-pack abs.

"There are no security devices activated. I paid the hostess to lock the entrance doors and she stated no males are inside. I hoped it would put you more at ease if I rented the entire facility while you're using it. No one else will know you were here. I'll stick close while you get acquainted with one of the bots. Just enter a room. They will ask you what you want." The father paused. "Take your time. We're not leaving the station until the next shift ends. You have twelve hours."

"Twelve hours. Understood." He marched to the first door. "Thank you." His begrudging tone belied that statement. "Just go. It will make this less embarrassing if you aren't here."

Venice sucked air into her starved lungs when the father left the lounge area and the tall, dusky male entered one of the brothel rooms. Her improved legs didn't buckle under her but she was pretty sure her old ones would have from the shock. She reached up and covered her mouth, holding back a gasp.

She'd never seen one before but the stories were legendary... stories about a race of gray-skinned cyborgs Earth Government had created before she'd been born. They had been some kind of failed program, and the government had told the public all the units had been destroyed. Rumors surfaced occasionally of sightings, but Earth Government always managed

12

to fill the news with proof that the sightings were lies, invented to keep people from venturing too far into deep space.

Cyborgs were obviously alive and well. The government had lied, but that didn't surprise her. And one of the cyborgs was a thirty-five-year-old virgin who couldn't get a woman to have sex with him.

Venice stumbled out from behind the large artificial vegetation and stared at the door he'd disappeared behind, her mind working through the astonishment. He had a father and they'd talked about children. That meant they were more man than machines. They could breed.

The automated brothel was closed for the evening until the next shift started, thanks to the man's father. It meant she was locked inside. Darbis's men wouldn't find her and she'd be safe until the cyborgs left.

The image of the handsome cyborg seemed burned into her mind. He was really attractive, big…and looked pretty kickass. They were obviously masquerading as pirates to avoid detection, and were in the same situation as Venice. Earth Government would want them dead if they were found or returned to the planet. Their very existence would prove EG had lied to the public.

She dropped her hand and smoothed down her shirt while still staring at the closed door the cyborg had entered. She tossed her weapon into the planter and hesitated a few seconds more, knowing she'd have to act quickly and there wouldn't be time to rethink her crazy plan once she'd implemented it. Her options were limited. She'd fled home and needed to do whatever was necessary to ensure her survival in space.

Go on and do it, she ordered her body. *Move!*

13

She touched the keypad and the door opened. She stepped inside the room before she could change her mind.

The sight of a stripping sex bot drew her attention first. The thing was tall, endowed, and strikingly beautiful, in the way only someone artificially created could be. Then her gaze shifted to the cyborg.

He'd removed most of his clothing—and that sight parted her lips. Muscles not only bulked up his arms, chest, and stomach, but they were thickly displayed on his powerful bared thighs. She stared at his tiny black underwear, which appeared to be leather, while trying to keep her mouth from dropping completely open. The budge there couldn't be hidden, actually pulled the tight material away from his skin. It was the most impressive sight she'd ever seen.

"I didn't request two," he gruffly muttered. "Were you ordered to come in here by another customer?"

She stared at his face. Those eyes of his were stunning. They did appear to be luminous; they were so bright blue compared to his darker skin hue, and gorgeous. She licked her lips and remembered to breathe. She had to find her voice.

"One is more than enough." He growled when he spoke again, frustration clear in his expression. "One of you needs to go."

He thinks I'm a sex bot. It left her speechless that he'd believe she was pretty enough to be one. She had taken care with her appearance before reaching the station, to impress her new husband. It was quite a compliment, though, if the cyborg believed she was in the same ranking as an artificial woman.

14

She turned her head to address the sex bot. "Leave. You are dismissed."

The bot followed orders. It left the room half naked without protest. Venice touched the pad to lock the door behind it, something she was grateful the cyborg hadn't done. Otherwise she wouldn't have been able to speak to him.

"The customer ordered an upgraded model," she lied. "I am here to service you."

"Great." He sat on the bed, reclined against the headboard and stretch out his long legs, and grumbled under his breath, "My dad thinks of everything. I've never been so uncomfortable in my life."

Sympathy welled inside Venice. She remembered the first time she'd had sex, and it had been a nightmare. She'd just wanted to be rid of her virginity. The young man she'd chosen had been cute but in a hurry to get her naked. It had gone downhill from there. Her choice turned out to be inept at sex, and it wasn't anything to brag about.

She wouldn't wish that memory on anyone. The handsome cyborg deserved a good experience, and she wanted to give it to him—especially if she had any hope of him helping her. She immediately walked over and sat on the bed next to him, trying to hide how he scared her because of his larger size. Her hand trembled as she rested her fingers on his arm. It was warm, firm, and felt nice.

"We can talk first. You should relax. It's going to be fine."

His head snapped in her direction and he frowned, staring at her. "What?"

"I'm an upgraded model," she lied. "I was just manufactured four months ago." That part was somewhat true. That's when she'd had the surgeries that had given her a new life. "I have a personality, and I was told this is your first time. We can go slowly."

"I'd rather get it over with." He glanced at her hand on his arm and cleared his throat. "I've always wanted to do this but none of the females were willing to test me out." He tenderly touched the back of her hand. "You're warm, and you feel alive."

"So do you."

His amazingly blue gaze held hers. "That's an odd thing to say. Are you reading that I'm something not human?" His mouth twisted with worry.

"It's polite conversation." She hoped that covered her slip. Sex bots wouldn't register a difference or know he was a cyborg. They weren't programmed to do so. "What is your name?"

He relaxed. "Deviant."

He had a strange name, and she hoped she hadn't just signed up for something really weird. She was willing to give him the benefit of the doubt though, since he'd admitted he'd never had sex. No one had tagged him with that nickname for his sexual practices.

"I'm Venice."

"That's pretty."

"Thank you. Would you like to talk first? It will be better if we get to know each other." *Stall and work up the courage to come clean with him.*

He rubbed her hand with his fingers, gently exploring it. "I'd rather just have sex." His cheeks darkened as she watched, embarrassment the obvious cause. "I'm really impatient to have this experience. I've spent a lot of years imagining it."

Indecision sparked in her mind, not sure how to go about getting what she needed from him. He might balk if she uttered the truth. He'd come to get laid, not to be burdened with someone who was in deep shit. But she desperately needed his help.

Maybe he'll agree if I show him what he could have.

That thought left her feeling more nervous, but he was sexy, as desperate as her, and they were both in a position to offer the other something. She'd spent over a month mentally preparing to sleep with the stranger she had proxy-married. *Different guy but you expected this. Just do it!*

She wasn't willing to straddle and ride him. Her body wasn't turned on enough, since fear was kind of a killer on her sex drive. The idea of him refusing what she wanted to propose was terrifying. Darbis's men would drag her back to his office and her life would turn hellish as soon as he sold her to the first customer—and it wouldn't be a blushing virgin. The customers would be pirates, or whatever other freaks could afford to pay for a breathing woman this far out in space.

It was a strong motivator to get down and dirty with the cyborg.

"Stretch out more and put your hands over your head."

He arched his eyebrows. "I don't know much but I think that's *my* line."

17

She nearly smiled, instantly more at ease, considering he had a sense of humor. It made her like him. "You wish to learn, correct? You've never done this before." She kept her voice calm despite her hammering heart. It could turn ugly fast if he didn't do what she wanted, and instead decided to pin her flat to do whatever *he* wanted. "You won't last long the first time."

His cheeks darkened again but she wasn't sure if it was a blush or if it was from anger. His tone clued her in though, and she relaxed.

"I have stamina but you might be accurate. I've heard from my friends that it feels really good."

He shifted his body to lay flat and reached up. He used his palms to cushion the back of his head and continued to watch her. His intense gaze narrowed and his chest rose and fell a little faster as his breathing increased with excitement.

"What next?"

Oh boy, she inwardly muttered. She'd never touched a stranger before, but then, she'd never found herself off Earth and trying to avoid becoming a whore, either. The cyborg had admitted to his father that other women didn't want him, but she found him attractive. He could protect her and get her off the station.

She wet her lips and she hoped he didn't notice that her hands trembled a little when she reached for his leather-like underwear. Her focus left his beautiful stare to study them.

"They unfasten on the side." He definitely breathed faster and his cock strained more against the material.

18

She found the hidden clasps and released one side. His cock broke free, rose straight to point upward, and she tried to smother a gasp. It was thick, long, the color a shade darker than his skin. He'd also been circumcised. No hair covered his lower abdomen or the apex of his thighs. He was completely hairless in that region.

Venice's hands shook more as she unfastened the other side of his strange underwear and let it fall to the bed. She licked her lips again. *This isn't going to be easy.* She studied his girth. It had been too many years since she'd had a lover but she hoped she hadn't forgotten the basics.

"Are you functioning properly?" His muscles tensed as he began to sit up.

She shot her hand out to flatten it on his lower belly, the muscles rock hard under his hot skin. She gave a sharp nod. "I am appreciating the sight." *And trying not to freak the hell out because you're huge.*

"You can skip that part." He relaxed. "My ego is fine but thank you."

It should be. Most guys would whip that bad boy out at parties just to make other men feel penis envy. And they would.

She schooled her thoughts and caressed his belly by trailing her hand lower.

His cock twitched and he softly groaned. "That feels wonderful."

She hadn't even gotten to the good part yet.

"Your hand is so soft and unlike my own."

That provided a mental image of him masturbating, which helped her libido flare to life. She'd bet her only pair of shoes that it would be a sexy

19

sight to watch him touch himself. She traced his upper thigh with her fingertips and he shifted a little on the bed, spreading his legs farther apart.

"I like this. I don't need to be turned-on more. I'm ready to go."

She wrapped her fingers around his shaft and his body jerked. A deep rumbling sound came from his throat. She glanced up to see his eyes squeezed closed as he bit his lower lip for a second.

"Fuck. I'm *not* going to last. I know it. I'm ready to come. Thank the stars you aren't a real female. I'd be humiliated."

If only you knew. She wet her lips again, glad he wasn't watching her, and leaned over him enough for her hair to spill across his hip. She didn't give him time to realize what she was going to do as she opened her mouth wide, hoped her teeth fit around him, and thanked her lucky stars that he was so attractive she actually *wanted* to do the deed.

Her tongue touched the crown of his cock where fluid glistened and surprise registered at the sweet taste. She licked him again as he moaned louder. It hid her gasp. He tasted kind of like maple syrup, an expensive Earth treat most people could only afford to buy for special-occasion breakfasts. He certainly wasn't human, and she was really glad for it as more of the taste coated her tongue. She sealed her lips around him, swirled her tongue, and took him deeper.

The bed moved and she lifted her gaze enough to see his hands grab at the bedding, fisting it, but he kept his hips locked down. She was grateful for that, or he'd likely choke her with the long length of his cock. Her hand gripped his shaft tighter, and she stroked him as she moved her mouth up and down, sucking and licking.

"Fuck," he rasped. "That's...amazing. Don't stop!"

She moved faster, could feel how steely rigid his cock grew, and the only warning he gave was crying out as he started to come. More of the sweet taste filled her mouth. She swallowed it down and slowed her mouth as she milked him.

His body shook, the bed with him, since he was so big. She finally eased off to lift her head. A sense of power hit her as she studied the sated, sexy cyborg. His eyes were closed as he panted. His hands still clawed the covers but he'd relaxed his death grip on them. A slow smile curved his generous mouth.

"Thank you," he rasped, and his eyes opened to stare at her. "You need to teach me how to please a woman orally, now that I know how wonderful it is to be the receiver of such enjoyment."

Temptation was there to strip out of her clothes and give him step-by-step instructions on how to make her scream his name. She presumed he'd be eager to learn, was smart enough to get it right, but he'd know she wasn't artificial if she allowed it. He might be a virgin, but he was too clever not to pick up any clues if the experience would be as mind-blowing as she suspected.

He sat up slowly as she released his cock, which was still mostly hard. He gave her a smile. It made him go from handsome to devastating. She took a seat next to him.

"Remove your clothes, stretch out on your back, and spread your thighs apart."

He gave her direct orders, his voice full of authority, and a sex bot would do it instantly. She hesitated and his smile faded.

"Are you having a problem with your audio sensors?"

She cleared her throat and took a breath, backing up more. "I need you to remain calm."

His gaze jerked to the door and concern tensed his features. "Was an alarm triggered? Has someone entered this section?" He rose to his feet in one fluid motion and grabbed something from his discarded pants on the floor. He came up holding a weapon gripped in his hand.

Shit! He thought they were being attacked. She remained seated. "Deviant? You can put down the weapon. Please? Don't shoot me."

He paused at the door, cocked his head, and seemed to be listening. He finally spared her a glance. "How many intruders? Are they other customers? Hook into the mainframe and get me the information."

"Deviant? No one is out there."

He lowered the weapon and turned fully to face her, the sight of the still turned-on, naked cyborg something striking to see. He was ready to do battle. Most guys would at least grab their pants but he'd only gone for his weapon. The thing was some kind of an odd-looking gun she'd never seen before, small enough to fit completely inside his fist.

"There's no danger out there. Could you please put down the weapon?"

"I won't shoot you." He actually moved his hand behind his ass cheek to hide it from her view. "There. Are you registering me as a nonthreat now?"

She stared into his eyes and wondered if he'd change his mind about shooting her when she told him the truth. Half of her was tempted to lie, tell him she was experiencing technical difficulties, and then send in a real bot. Of course, that would leave her stranded on the station and screwed in a really bad way—by many customers.

"I'm in serious trouble, Deviant. I need your help."

He stalked forward with grace, bent enough to drop the weapon on his discarded clothing, and straightened. His hand gripped his cock and a grin curved his mouth.

"I've got exactly what you need." He winked. "I've heard of this dialog foreplay, and I'm going to help you, beautiful."

She was too stunned that he'd gone from one extreme to another to even react when he released his cock and dropped to his knees before her. His hands gripped her thighs, shoved them apart, and his chest hit hers. She was pinned under him on the bed in the next breath, staring into the face inches from her own. He gripped her wrists to jerk them above her head.

"I'll pay for the clothing. I'm going to tear them off."

Her heart pounded and she lifted her legs, wrapped them around his waist, the only thing she could grip. Her skirt had risen up; her bare legs touched his hot skin, and she shivered a little because it was kind of sexy, even if she *was* too afraid to fully appreciate it. Her arms strained to get loose but she couldn't break his one-handed hold, even with her improved left arm. He was stronger than the mechanics inside her.

"Should I kiss your mouth first or tear off your clothes to explore your breasts? Which do females prefer?"

"I'm a real person, Deviant. I'm not a sex bot." She said it quickly, afraid he'd act before she had a chance to answer his question.

"I like that." He leaned closer, his nose brushing hers, and closed his eyes. "Open your mouth to me now."

He smelled of mint, something he'd obviously eaten. She opened her mouth to tell him this wasn't part of some programmed dialog, a fantasy so clients could pretend she was real. She was being honest.

His lips sealed over hers and his tongue swept inside her mouth before she got a single word out.

For a virgin, the guy didn't kiss like one. He mastered her mouth easily, coaxed her tongue to move with his. Her body responded to the passion he ignited with his hungry exploration. Her legs shifted higher to his waist, her calves squeezed against his muscular, firm ass, and he rubbed the hard length of his cock against her panties to massage her clit.

She moaned, the sensation turning her on. It had been a really long time since anyone had touched her down there. Fire ignited inside her belly, burned from her sex upward, until it hazed over her ability to think. His strong hips rocked faster against the cradle of her thighs, firmly stroking his rigid cock against the thin material covering her pussy. She pressed back, seeking more contact.

He rumbled, his chest vibrated, and he released her wrists to brace one arm on the bed while his free hand gripped her shirt from the side. The material tightened over her rib cage and only the sound of it tearing jerked her from her fervent stupor.

Venice twisted her head away from his hungry mouth, broke the kiss, panting. Deviant's hips didn't pause their torturous stroking against her clit. His mouth focused on the column of her neck instead as his hot lips traced it with a few flicks of his tongue.

"Stop," she begged. "Wait."

His brush of kisses paused. "No. I'm going to fuck you until I can't move. We have eleven hours and forty-two minutes. I'm keeping track." He opened his mouth and nipped her shoulder. "But I like the coy act. It's turning me on more."

A jolt of desire shot through her at the way he bit her again. It wasn't painful, but instead made her wonder how it would feel on her nipples. They ached, along with the rest of her. She also knew if she didn't stop this now that he would follow through with his plan. She wouldn't mind...but it might piss him off more when he learned the truth. She needed his help too desperately to take that chance.

He arched his back, his mouth trailed down her collarbone, and he put a little space between their bodies to give his hands room to reach up and grip the vee of her shirt. He tore it open, baring her breasts, and his scorching mouth instantly sucked a nipple inside.

Venice cried out at the sheer pleasure. Things were moving super-fast, and damned if she didn't want him. She did. Her clit throbbed painfully, her vaginal muscles clenched as she hovered on the brink of climax.

Oh, screw it, she decided as her hands clutched at his hair. "Don't stop," she moaned. Her fingers dug into the silky strands, cupped the back of his head, and she hoped he wouldn't move away as he sucked harder on her nipple. His teeth scraping the oversensitive bud became sweet torture.

He rolled his hips, pushed his cock tighter against her clit, and rocked faster, with more force. The bed swayed from his strength and that did it for Venice. She shouted out as ecstasy seized her body. She was pretty sure she'd said his name but wasn't one hundred percent certain since it was a huge blur of bliss.

He tore his mouth away and hovered over her face, staring down at her with those electric-blue eyes. His features seemed darker than they had been before as he breathed heavily. Her gaze dropped to his lips, swollen from their kissing and what his mouth had done to her breast. It was a sexy sight, but she admitted to being biased after the shattering pleasure he'd just given her.

His hips stilled as her body trembled from the aftermath, and he growled at her. "Tell me the truth. Is that the exact reaction of a living female? Did I do it right?"

She was speechless.

"Foreplay is an art, and I know I am supposed to engage in penetration once you've reach sexual release. Which feels better for them? Do I tear off your panties? Enter you this way, on your back, or flip you over onto your knees to take you from behind? Which position hits a female's G-spot easier?"

Her hands shook as she realized he wouldn't believe the truth. He was certain she was a sex box sprouting programmed lines. In truth, the idea of him doing *either* of those things to her made Venice ache again. She'd bet he'd be good in any position—but she really needed off the station. Anything else they did together would only make him angrier when he finally realized she wasn't a bot.

But how do I show him?

She lowered her hands between them, knew it would hurt, but used the synthetic fingernails of her left hand to claw her right palm. Tears filled her eyes when she painfully broke the skin.

Confusion widened his eyes at the sight of Venice hurting herself, but she turned her bleeding skin enough for him to see.

"I'm real, Deviant. I'm not a bot and this isn't programming. That's blood. Look. I am *really* in trouble—and I need your help."

He stared at her hand and his mouth fell open. Total shock paled his dark features, and those pretty eyes of his flew up to stare deeply into hers.

In the next instant, he lifted off her with amazing speed, his weight gone, and she had a weapon pointed at her face from where he stood above her.

She glanced between the weapon and his stiff cock, pointing her way too. She swallowed down some of her terror that he might kill her, remained perfectly still, and forced her focus up his muscled body to meet his angry gaze.

"Please don't kill me. I have a proposition for you. Hear me out."

Chapter Two

"Who are you?" Deviant's tone was rough, cold, and deadly.

"Venice." She blinked, but that was all that moved besides her chest as she breathed, ignoring the blood dripping from her hand into the valley between her breasts. "Could you pretty please stop pointing that thing at my face?" She flickered her gaze to his gun, back to his erect cock, and then to his face, deciding she should clarify. "The gun."

His hold tightened. "You have one minute to explain who you are and what your mission is here before I pull the trigger. Are you an Earth spy or a soldier sent here to locate us?"

Terror gripped her. "I'm altered, three limbs and some of my internal organs." She babbled but it didn't matter as long as he didn't kill her. "I'm as screwed as you are with Earth Government if they get their hands on me. I—"

"Altered how?"

She didn't point out it was rude to cut her off while she was trying to explain, and that he was wasting precious seconds of the time she'd been given. "I was in a horrible accident. The damage was too severe for normal treatment, and Earth Government locked me inside a holding facility to die. There's a law on Earth that if a certain percentage of you is damaged, it's illegal to make the repairs. You're considered nonhuman at that point. The only reason they didn't kill me outright was because I have a rare blood type. They kept me locked up for four years while they used me to produce blood to sell. Scientists can make both artificial and cloned blood but...rich people like to buy the genuine thing."

She sucked in a gulp of air. "My sister hired a hacker to enter the facility's database, when she grew suspicious after they refused to give her my remains. Other people get their families' bodies to burn but she wasn't given anything. She saw photos of the accident and knew there should have been remains." She sucked in another breath.

"Slow down."

"You said I only had a minute."

"I'll give you longer if you make more sense." He shifted his stance but didn't lower the weapon.

"Okay." She paused. "My sister discovered where I was being held, what they were doing to me, and hired Angels to steal me."

"Angels?" His gaze narrowed. "As in the religious context?"

"They're a group of people who believe it's wrong for the government to just make people disappear, and or use them for profit. Angels is the organization's name. They try to rescue those who've been deemed too damaged to save, and break into facilities to find people like me, who are used to harvest body parts, internal organs, or blood for rich people. They got me out of there and took me to an underground medical facility, where they performed surgeries to attach three artificial limbs. They also replaced my damaged organs with manufactured ones, and a few of my bones had to be replaced as well. They put skin grafts on my burns to get rid of the scars." She paused and tried to think of what else to say that might save her life.

29

"Go on."

"I could have registered as an artificial life form, and tried to hide as my sister's 'property,' but all the work on me is illegal, since it was done by an underground movement. That means I'll be destroyed if I'm caught, same as if I were a homemade android someone put together. All artificial life forms are considered slaves, and you have to pay to have them built by one of the regulated, licensed companies approved by the government. The law doesn't care that I'm a live person. I'm over the percentage of manufactured parts allowed, and that means I'm not considered human. Unless, you know, you're rich or come from a powerful family with serious connections to obtain a waiver. They can afford to bribe officials to bypass the laws. I had to flee Earth as soon as I recovered."

He watched her as the silence stretched between them.

"They scan everyone, everywhere on Earth. My true identity would have alerted the authorities that I should be dead or still locked inside the facility. A more in detailed body scan would have revealed how much of me is altered, and they would have immediately arrested me. That would have been a death sentence. I came *here* thinking I'd be safe, but that was all bullshit. I need your help, and as I said, I have a proposition for you."

"What?" He snarled the word.

"Take me off this station when you leave. I was hiding in the waiting room when you and your dad entered. I, um…overheard what you two talked about. We can help each other. You need a woman, and technically I *am* one." She forced a smile. "I need to go somewhere I won't be abused or arrested. You get me, and I get a safe place to live."

He stared at her.

She lowered her gaze, saw he was still aroused, and hope flared.

"You want me. You can have me. And I'll teach you whatever you want to know. Just *please* get me off this station."

"Why?"

She swallowed. "Because you like me. I mean, you *seem* interested..." She glanced at his cock again. "I—"

"Why do you need off this station? This isn't Earth. They don't run scans here. We wouldn't visit it if they did."

"Oh. That." She eased up very slowly until she sat, keeping her hands in his view to avoid being shot if he thought she posed a threat. "I needed to get off Earth fast, once my surgeries were done and I'd healed enough to travel. I'd heard about how many deep-space traders were looking for wives. Convincing a real woman to move this far out is tough, you know. Most women don't want to live so far from civilization, and it's kind of crazy dangerous with all the pirate attacks." She paused. "Of course, that seemed tame to me, considering an entire planet wants me captured and destroyed. So I logged onto the deep-space bride registry and thought I'd found a husband."

"The what?" He actually lowered his weapon a few inches.

"Deep-space bride registry. It's where women put ads to find husbands who live this far out, and men answer them if they want a wife. I found this guy, and even told him the truth about what happened to me. He knew why I needed to leave Earth. I wanted to be honest, and I planned to be a real wife to him. He was giving me a new chance at life by saving me from certain death." She licked her lips. "It turns out he lied to me. The guy I talked to is just an employee, who was impersonating my *real* husband—a troll who marries women from Earth, gets them out here, and forces them to work in his private brothel."

"Troll?"

"It's a derogatory name for a big ugly jerk. He's much older than he stated, covered in warts, and just gross." She hesitated. "Please get me off this station, Deviant. I'll do whatever you want. I just have a few demands."

His eyebrows rose as his eyes widened. "*You* have demands?"

"Yes." She winced. "I know how that sounds, but I'm trying to escape so I'm not turned into a whore. I'd like you to promise that you won't do that to me."

Deviant took a step closer. "You aren't a paid sex worker?"

"No." She glanced at the bed and then him. "Um, this was my first time."

"You're a virgin?"

"No!" She was making a mess out of this. "I mean, I've had sex before, but never for money. Technically, you didn't just pay me to blow you. I meant that I don't work here. I came in here to show you that...oh hell." Tears filled her eyes. "Could you put the gun down? Please don't shoot me. I'm desperate!"

He hesitated before grabbing his pants and shoving them on. He slid his gun into the holster attached to his waist as he crouched down a foot away from her. His blue eyes were amazing as they locked onto hers. "I'm confused."

"So am I." She wiped at her tears. "I just wanted a new life, and instead I came here to find out the guy who'd married me doesn't exist. I was tricked by this asshole, who wants to turn me into a whore, and then I saw you, and you're totally hot; I don't know why women from wherever you're from won't touch you. I want you to take me with you, Deviant. I just don't want to be forced to sleep with other guys. I'll have sex with *you* though, if you save me."

He blinked.

"That's what my conditions are. You want a woman who'll have sex with you, and that's what I'm offering. I just don't want to be passed around to other men. Is that clear enough? I haven't had sex in over four years, since before my accident." She bit her lip. "I was afraid I'd even forgotten *how* to give a blow job. Was it at least good for you?"

He slowly rose to his full height. "Stand up."

She trembled but stood. The guy was a good foot taller than her. He reached out and gripped the hand she'd cut, turned it to stare at her palm. His gaze shifted to hers. "This arm is the real one? You mentioned three of your limbs were replaced."

"Yeah. Both legs and my other arm had to be added."

He stared into her eyes. "Organs?"

"A kidney and a lung. Most of my rib cage was replaced. One shoulder blade isn't the original either."

"Give me your other hand."

33

She lifted her other one and he took it, tracing her palm with his fingers. It tickled and she jerked a little in his hold. He gave her a questioning look.

"It's really sensitive. Angels use the best materials they can and it's very lifelike. I feel pain and everything."

"It feels very real. I can't tell the difference by touch." He hesitated. "What about your breasts and your vagina? Are those real or replacements?"

"Real and totally my original parts."

He leaned in to stare at her face. "Enhanced?"

"A little. I had burns on one side, but they put lab-grown skin over the worst of it to match the other side of my face, and repair all the damage. This is how I looked before my accident, more or less."

"What about your hair color? Is that soft brown what you were born with?"

"Yes."

"How old are you?"

"Thirty."

His minty breath fanned her face. "I don't even know what to do with you."

Hope flared. "Take me with you, help me escape, and I'll teach you everything you ever wanted to learn about a woman's body. That's why you came here, right? I'm sexually attracted to you. You were attracted to *me*. Is my being real a bad thing?"

He released her hands. "Who's after you?"

"The station owner. His name is Darbis Martin, and he's a son of a bitch. A real bad guy. He bragged about doing this to other women before me. He's got a private brothel with live women on this station too. I ran before he could have me escorted there. That's when I saw you."

He backed up a few feet and regarded her with a frown. "How long?"

"I just got here today."

"I meant, how long will I own you if I get you off this station?"

Own me? Yikes. She swallowed. "How long do you want to keep me?"

"Where do you want to go after you work off your debt to me, if I take you away from this place?"

Her mind blanked. "I don't know. I have no idea where I'd be safe. I thought it was safe *here*, but I was wrong."

Deviant watched her for a long moment.

"Please?" she pleaded. "All I ask, besides you taking me away from here, is that you be the only one to touch me. I'm not a whore."

"You're completely willing to give me your body?"

She let her gaze travel over him. "Yes. That's not really a hardship, Deviant." She saw his surprised look and smiled. "Are the women where you come from blind?"

"You're lying to me. I'm not attractive."

It was her turn to be surprised when total sincerity shone in his eyes. "They *must* be blind. You're hot, Deviant."

He frowned.

"You've got the best body I've ever seen and your eyes are so beautiful. Um, you're built…all over." She hesitated. "And you taste really good. On Earth, I'd have had to pay a month's salary for that."

He paled. "What?"

"You taste like maple syrup. It's a very expensive, sweet treat on Earth."

He was speechless.

"I prefer telling the truth. Maybe that was *too* much honesty." She knew her cheeks were turning pink. "Forget I said that last part. Take me with you and you can keep me for as long as you want. Just promise that you're the only man who touches me. I'm a good cook and easy to live with." She forced a smile. "I know a lot of jokes. I won't be a burden. I don't even eat much."

He took deep breaths and finally sighed. "Remove your skirt."

"Um, okay." She nodded, reaching behind her to unzip it. Her cheeks warmed more. "You want to get a look at what you're bargaining for. I get it." She pushed her skirt down and stood there in her panties and torn-open shirt. She hesitated but then shoved the damaged shirt away since, he could already see her breasts. Her gaze lifted and she took a deep breath, trying to calm her racing heart. "Should I turn around?"

His brilliant blue eyes slowly traveled the length of her body. "Come here." He pointed to the floor in front of him.

She kicked out of her skirt tangled at her ankles and approached him. Embarrassment at being studied that closely flared, but she fought it down. The guy had the right to see what he was risking his ass for. It probably

36

wouldn't be easy to get her off the station, what with Darbis's men searching it. She stopped in front of him and he cupped her jaw with his hand, making her look up at him.

"You're shy. It wasn't an act, you being coy in bed, was it?" His voice had deepened and turned husky.

She didn't know what to say but she held his gaze.

"You said it's been four years since you had sex. How many males have you tested in your bed?"

"Tested?"

"How many have entered your body?"

"Three."

His eyebrows rose. "Three?"

She blushed more. "I know that sounds bad but the first guy didn't count. I wanted to get rid of my virginity. Everyone knows when you're a virgin because of the detailed, full-body scans at work, to make certain you aren't stealing anything. The guards always snickered when I passed through, and joked about it. I kind of slept with the first guy I could, just to get rid of it. The second guy I liked, but he lied to me. I don't date pilots, and he was one, but he said he worked food services." She paused. "The third guy…I was engaged to him before my accident. I looked him up when I was freed but he'd married someone else. I guess he'd thought I'd died and had moved on."

"You said the first one didn't count, so who are you not telling me about?"

"That's it. I just meant it wasn't like real sex. It was just to get rid of my virginity."

"Then why would that sound bad? I'm confused."

She hesitated. "I know that sounds like a lot of men."

Eyebrows arched. "Three?"

She nodded.

He stared deeply into her eyes. "I will be the only one who touches you. You'll belong to me until I feel your debt has been paid, but I'll treat you well. Do you agree to my terms?"

"Yes. Just get me off this station. *Please*."

He let her go. "Stand on the bed."

Venice turned and wondered why he wanted her up there, but figured it might be a test to see if she'd follow his orders. She lifted her leg, stepped on the bed, and stood still on the mattress. She turned to face him, surprised to find him right behind her.

He suddenly gripped her hips. "I have to figure a way to get you off this station. You can't very well walk next to me as we leave."

She finally understood. "You plan to carry me?"

"I don't see any other choice. They will probably stop anyone your size walking through the station." His arms opened. "Wrap around me."

Her fingers gripped his shoulders and he grabbed her hips, lifted her right off her feet as if she didn't weigh a thing, and jerked her against his body. She wrapped her legs around his waist, and stared into his eyes inches from her own.

"You're small but not small enough." He frowned. "Release me."

She let him go and he had her stand on the bed again. He took a few steps back, studied her, and frowned. "I don't suppose your limbs come off easily and reattach?"

"No!" The idea shocked her.

A faint grin curved his handsome mouth. "That would have been convenient. I had to ask. Give me a moment. I'll think of something."

"You could put me in a bag and carry me over your shoulder. They'll think I'm merchandise."

"That would be too suspicious if they are searching for you, and they might be checking anything large enough to contain a human." His gaze traveled all over her, making her feel warm. Then he looked away to glance around the room.

He moved toward the fake window curtains that were part of the decoration, tore one of them off the wall, and turned. "I have an idea. This might not be comfortable for you, but it won't last for long."

"I can deal with it." She shrugged. "It's going to beat being forced into sexual slavery."

He froze.

"I didn't mean with *you*. I meant staying here and having to work in that brothel."

"You're lucky we dress as pirates, and their garb is very loose."

"That's definitely a bonus right now."

He flashed a grin. "Stand up."

She climbed to her feet, wondering what he'd do with the material. He stepped forward, holding the curtain in one hand, and then grabbed her around her waist, jerking her against his firm body. Their gazes locked.

"Put your arms beneath mine and grip my shoulders from behind."

She did, curving her fingers around his warm skin. He had expansive shoulders, and her tight hold on him flattened her breasts against his muscled chest. Her heart accelerated and the blue of his eyes seemed to darken again while they watched each other.

"Wrap your legs around my waist. Hold on to me tight to support your own weight for a moment."

She did, and it was like hugging a muscled tree. His arm slid from around her waist to hook under her ass, jerked her tight against his pelvis, and she realized his cock was hard, trapped between their bellies.

"Don't move."

She didn't as he released her, used both arms to spread the curtain, and began to wrap it around their bodies. She quickly got what he was doing as he wound the material, forcing her legs to hug him even tighter. He tore each end of the curtain into short strips after he wrapped it around their bodies, and tied the strips together. His hands gripped her hips, he wiggled his body a little, and she slipped down him a few inches.

"Tuck your head against my chest."

She did it, pressing her cheek against him. Her ear flattened, she could hear his firm, strong heartbeat. His arms wrapped around her back and he sighed.

"This will have to do. Don't move."

40

"I can't. You have me wrapped too tight."

"Good." He held her as he bent, grabbed his shirt and head gear, and straightened. "It's about to get worse. You can't speak or move, do you understand me?"

"Yes."

He put the shirt on and covered her body with it. He probably looked pretty paunchy with her over his front, but the loose clothing still didn't seem to suffer from tightness. The shirt fell almost to his knees. When he put on the head drape, she lost sight of all light. It was dark and warm, hard to breathe, and her ankles protested being twisted a little, and wrapped so tightly against his body. It wasn't outright painful though. It was just really awkward having her knees up by his ribs.

He took a deep breath—it made her hold hers—and he blew it out. "Hold very still. I'll hurry, and we might make it off the station without suspicion. Whatever happens, hold on to my shoulders and don't let go. Are you strong enough?"

"Yes," she assured him. "I'm desperate and terrified of being caught. I can hang on for however long it takes."

His arms wrapped around her in a brief hug. "It won't be long. My ship isn't docked too far from here."

He opened the door and had to release her with one arm to do it. She realized that every step he took rubbed his thick, hard shaft against her spread pussy and stomach. He pulled her ass even tighter against his hips and held her weight with his arm. She bit her lip and understood that the real torture wasn't going to be wrapped up like a mummy against the big

41

cyborg. It was going to be not moaning as he picked up his pace, strode faster, and her pussy ground against his cock.

Hell. That's what I'm in. She bit her lip to prevent a moan from passing her lips, squeezed her eyes closed, and tried to concentrate on holding on to his shoulders.

"I have to let you go," he rasped when he paused. "We're leaving the automated brothel." His arm released her and she tightened her hold on him. "Hang on, Venice."

The sounds of the station were instant when the door slid open. Men's voices, the drone of machines, and music filled the ear not pressed tight to Deviant's chest. His heart rate increased, telling her he was either afraid or just under some strain from walking with her extra weight. He didn't seem to have much trouble with the latter. He moved fast, his cock rubbing against her clit with every long step. She wondered if he was having the same issue she had.

Her clit throbbed and pleasure made her tense. She bit her lip, hugged him tighter, and didn't dare try to lift her body higher up his to escape the thick mass of his dick. It was trapped between their bodies in the perfect spot, and every step bounced her a little, making her ride his cock as it slid over her clit. Up. Down. Up. Down.

Oh shit, she frantically thought. *Don't come. Don't. Your life is in danger. Is it just me or is his dick harder? Shit! He's harder...he just stumbled a little.*

42

His body hit something. He paused and hissed out a curse above her. His breathing was harsher but she wasn't sure if it was from carrying her or because he was suffering the same fate she was—sexual torment.

A hand suddenly gripped her ass, squeezed hard, and she was crushed between something solid, unforgiving, and his body. He took a deep breath, released her ass, and shoved away from the surface he'd pressed her against. She didn't have to see it to know it was a wall. He walked again, moving faster.

Up. Down. Up. Down. Her clit throbbed, she grit her teeth, and pleasure tormented her. Her nails dug into his skin; she couldn't help it. She frantically tried to resist but the slide of his cock against her ultra-sensitive bundle of nerves won out. She held her breath, but that only made it worse, and her climax tore through her.

She thought she might faint. Her body jerked a little against his and she prayed no one was looking at him when it happened. He uttered a soft curse but she heard it as he kept going. Blackness came at her and she forced a little air into her lungs to avoid passing out. Her clit was so sensitive, her vaginal muscles twitched, and she knew pure hell for real. She nearly lost her grip on his shoulders but managed to cling.

He jerked to a halt suddenly, swung to the left, and her back came up against something solid again. He was breathing heavy. Both of his hands grabbed her ass through layers of material and he ground his cock against her hard, thrusting his hips in short, jerky movements, and then groaned softly as his body shook. Warmth spread through his pants to her belly, and she knew he'd just come himself.

"You're going to pay for that," he rasped a few seconds later.

Her mouth opened but before she could speak, he jerked away from the wall, released her ass, and walked again. His cock softened though, easing her torment, since he wasn't rigidly rubbing up against her swollen clit anymore.

Something bumped them jarringly, his body swayed a little, and someone loudly snarled a curse.

"Watch it," Deviant growled back in a chilling voice.

"Damn drunk," someone muttered. "You bumped into *me*, you mutated asshole."

They walked a little farther before Deviant stopped yet again. He brushed a hand against her ass, removed something from a pocket lower down his leg, and she heard a door slide open. He took a few more steps.

"We're clear but not safe yet. Hang on, Venice. You okay?"

"Yes," she whispered.

Sweat tickled between their bodies where their chests and bellies were smashed together. The sensation of rising quickly made her dizzy and she wondered if they'd entered some kind of lift. She had no idea where they were but the rising sensation ceased. Deviant was walking, doors swished open and closed, and he finally stopped.

Light showed through her closed eyelids when he stretched his arms upward, and she opened her eyes as fresh air hit her. He'd thrown off his head drape, and struggled out of the shirt next.

Venice sucked in heavy breaths and pulled away from his chest, her face felt nearly glued to it after their adventure. She blinked a few times to adjust to the bright lights.

"Welcome to your new home," he sighed.

She stared at the living quarters. It wasn't big, maybe fifteen by nine feet, with a bed in one corner and a cleansing unit in another. Books lined one shelf along an entire wall, the spines printed in some weird language she'd never seen before. She turned to stare at the cyborg who'd rescued her.

"I'm going to fuck you just as soon as I shower." He frowned. "I've never come in my pants before. That's classified information. Do you understand me? Don't ever tell anyone that happened."

She nodded, stunned.

He stepped over to his bunk—a long, narrow one—and reached up to a shelf high above it. She gasped when he grabbed a sharp-looking blade. He paused as she stared at him with fear, wondering what he planned to do with it.

"Don't move."

He cut the curtain that wrapped them together, the sharp metal slashing through it easily, but he skillfully avoided her skin. The second the pressure was off, her legs slid down his body. Her ass landed on a soft mattress when he backed away.

"Stay," he ordered. "If you try to run, you won't be thrilled with what you find out there."

Her gaze left his and located the door. She stared back up at him.

"You're on a ship full of cyborgs. No one knows you're here, and for right now, I want to keep it that way. So do you."

She licked her lips. "Okay. I won't try to run from you. You saved me."

He crouched down, staring into her eyes. "They'll want me to share you. Do you understand? You're the only female on a ship with seven males."

Fear hit hard.

An emotion akin to pity flashed in his eyes as he reached out and cupped her cheek. "I'm the only one who will touch you, but you need to follow my rules. Don't try to leave this room. I can protect you here." He glanced at the door before staring into her eyes again. "I'm going to shower. Get ready for me."

"Okay."

He released her and stood. She watched him step into the cleansing unit before the door closed, and she was alone. Seconds later it turned on, but Venice just sat there.

"Did I just get myself into worse trouble?"

No one answered her.

Chapter Three

The second the cleansing unit shut off, Venice scrambled to remove her underwear, wishing she could use Deviant's shower too. He wasn't the only one who'd gotten off during their walk to his ship. Her panties were soaked from both times he'd made her come. She used a dry part of them to wipe off her tummy where he'd left his seed and balled up the evidence, looking around the tidy room. She didn't have a clue where to put them. He didn't have a hamper or a trash can. And it was the only piece of clothing she had left.

She turned and shoved them under his pillow, taking a seat.

The unit opened and a wet, mostly naked Deviant stood there. She stared, her mouth open, suddenly reminded how sexy he was. The towel wrapped around his waist rode low enough to show off his flat, firm belly. Muscles were apparent in a tight group of ridges—and that wasn't the only muscle she saw. His cock was hard, trapped under the material hugging his thighs. She lifted her gaze.

Bright blue eyes met hers before they lowered to her body. He stepped out of the small cleaning area and into his room. There wasn't much space between the wall and the bunk. He reached for the towel, dropped it on the floor, and his cock lifted. Her heart raced and she knew what he wanted. He'd already told her.

"You owe me. I wasn't going to take time to get dry, so I hope you don't mind me in this state."

"You saved me."

"I'm talking about how we got here. You came, didn't you?"

She nodded. "You were rubbing up against me. I tried to fight it but…it felt too good."

"Lay back and spread your thighs. Show me."

His husky tone turned her on. She twisted on the bed, scooted until she could lean back and rest her head on his pillow. It smelled like him, masculine and nice. She lifted her thighs, parted them wide, and placed her feet flat along the edges of the bunk. The wall was cool where one of her knees rested.

She couldn't look away from the cyborg who took a seat near the end of the bed. His sole focus was on her sex.

"So pink and small," he rasped.

"Have you ever seen a woman this way before?" She remembered he was a virgin.

"Not in person." He leaned over, studying her pussy, and then reached for her.

She shivered when his finger traced her slit. She was really wet, and she sucked in air when his fingertip explored her clit. He paused and his gaze lifted. He arched one eyebrow.

Teach him, she reminded herself. *That's what he wants.* "That's the most sensitive spot." She reached down, her fingers spreading her vaginal lips more, and gave him a better view. "You want to learn, right?"

"Yes." His voice came out deeper.

"Do you want to learn oral first or just fuck me to know what it feels like?"

"You look so delicate. I'm afraid I'll hurt you."

"If you were to just enter me fast and hard without me being turned-on, it would hurt. You're big, Deviant." She lifted her head and stared at his erect cock. "Really big."

His finger lowered to her slit again and tested it by pressing slightly inside her vaginal opening. "I wouldn't fit inside you here."

"Yes, you will. We're designed to stretch. Feel how wet I am? It helps to ease you inside me."

"I want to fuck you."

"Okay." She hesitated. "Do you mind if I'm on top at first?"

He pulled away from her and sat up. "Teach me how to do this so it feels really good for a female."

Her level of arousal instantly shot up. Most guys would have crawled over her and gone to town, but this guy wanted it to be good for her. She sat up and studied him. "Sit back against the wall."

He did, and she couldn't help but get even more aroused by the fact that the big, sexy guy was doing what she told him to do. She had always wanted to try a few things, and suddenly she had a willing, hot man ready to do her bidding. He was damn near perfect.

She got to her knees, bit her lip, and then straddled his thighs, facing away. She saw surprise on his face as she turned her head to stare back at him. His gaze dropped to her ass and desire darkened the color of them. It wasn't her imagination. They slightly changed with his moods.

She reached between them and gripped his thick shaft. He sucked in air and lifted his gaze to hers. "I haven't read about this position. Is it an Earth one?"

"It's easier for me to ease onto you if I'm on top, to adjust to how big you are, and you can reach me better too if I'm facing away from you. Remember my clit? That sensitive spot?"

He nodded. "Yes."

"I'm going to lower down on you. I'm wet and ready to take you. Hold real still. In other words, don't drive up into me, even if you get the urge. When I'm riding you, reach around me and rub my clit. Up and down feels really good, or in circles. Wet your finger first."

His eyebrows arched but he licked his lips. "I understand."

She spread her thighs a bit, leaned back so her ass pressed against his firm stomach, and lifted his cock to line up with her pussy. The crown brushed her and she fought back a moan. Excitement hit her at what they were about to do, and she adjusted her hips to align them perfectly. She kept her head turned, watching his face.

"Ready?"

"Yes." His voice was really deep now, thick with desire.

Yeah, the women on his planet are blind, she decided. Deviant was so sexy, she was hurting to ride him. She lowered her hips, the tip of his thick shaft pushed against her, and she watched his mouth press into a tight line as his eyes narrowed. She pushed down. His cock was so stiff, her body parting for him readily, and she moaned as her vaginal walls stretched.

"Fuck," he growled.

"We're about to."

His hands gripped her hips. "You're so tight."

"That's just the head." She put more weight down and closed her eyes. "Oh God. You're big."

"Am I hurting you?"

She shook her head, too lost in the wonderful sensation of him filling her to speak. She lifted up a little, eased down, and took even more of him. His fingers squeezed her hips but he remained still otherwise. She moved up and down, taking more of him with every downward motion, until her ass rested against his hips. He was buried inside her deep, a part of her in every sense, and she'd never felt so taken in her life.

"Heaven," he rasped. "Don't stop."

"Play with my clit. Please!"

He released her hip and did as she asked. His chest pressed firmly against her back as he sat up and his fingers explored her pussy. He touched where they were connected, moved upward, and located the swollen flesh.

"Oh yeah..."

"What do I do?" He turned his head and lowered it, brushing a kiss against her neck.

"Small, tight circles."

"Understood."

He moved his finger—and then she knew heaven too. "Oh God."

"Like this?"

"Yes! Perfect." She started to move her hips, fucking him slowly. "You feel so good, Deviant."

"So do you. You're tight and wet. You squeeze my dick with each movement."

She rocked her hips faster, grinding down on his lap, and he applied more pressure against her clit without being asked.

"I'm going to come if you kiss and bite lightly at my neck," she moaned. "And pinch my nipples with your other hand."

He lifted his arm, hugging her against his body, and then cupped her breast right as his mouth found the side of her throat. His wet tongue teased her, his finger taunted her clit, and he used his thumb and finger to pinch the nipple of the breast he cupped with one big palm.

She went wild on his lap, bucking up and down, frantic now, and when he bit her, she lost it. Pure ecstasy shot through her body as she came hard, cried out his name, and seized on his lap.

Deviant cursed, released her breast, and his hand tore away from her pussy. He grabbed her hips, clutched them, and lifted Venice high before slamming her back down on his cock. He moved her fast, driving in and out of her during the height of her pleasure. He shouted out as he started to shoot his semen inside her.

She could feel him, hot jets filling her, and her twitching muscles milked him as she came down from her climax. His arms wrapped around her waist and he hugged her against his body as they both tried to catch their breath. She leaned her head against his shoulder, turning it to brush a kiss on his neck.

He adjusted them, strong enough to move with her body on top of his, and hugged her tighter. Venice liked that he held her afterward. She knew she had to move off him soon but wasn't in a hurry to break the intimate connection.

"You enjoyed that."

"I did."

"It wasn't a question." He turned his head enough to peer into her eyes. "Do you always need stimulation to your clitoris to climax?"

"I do. I hear some women don't."

He frowned. "How do I know if a woman does or not?"

She hesitated. "Ask?"

His gaze narrowed. "You aren't an expert, are you?"

"I never claimed to be."

His hold on her adjusted and he hugged her waist. "You're real though."

"Mostly."

"And you're mine."

"Yes." For as long as he wanted her. That was the deal. She didn't mention that part.

"We'll figure it out together."

"Okay."

"I'm a cyborg."

"I knew that. The gray skin gave it away," she admitted.

"Do I terrify you?"

"Do I look scared?" She smiled. "You did make me scream though."

He suddenly laughed. It was a great sound, and his features took her breath away when he did it, once again striking her how handsome he was. His hands started to explore her ribs, rose up to cup her breasts, and she softly moaned.

"Does that feel good?"

"Yes."

"I want to touch you all over."

"Go right ahead."

"I should warn you of something."

She stared into his eyes. "What is it?"

"Being a cyborg means I have stamina. I could fuck you a lot, Venice."

She shivered as he lightly pinched her nipples. "That doesn't scare me."

"Good." His hands slid down her ribs, over her stomach to her thighs. "I want to do you in every position I can think of."

"I'm all for that."

"I want to learn oral sex."

"I'm *really* all for that."

He chuckled. "I enjoyed you giving it, but it's my turn."

"Let me shower first. I want to get clean."

"Are you hungry?"

"Starving. I haven't eaten since whenever this morning was."

"I'll get you food while you use the cleansing unit. You will eat when I return with your meal, and afterward I want you spread out on my bed."

"That sounds like a terrific plan." His thumb brushed her clit and she arched her back. "I love you touching me."

"Good. I'm going to be doing it a lot. We have a few days before we reach my home world." He gripped her hips. "I'll get you food. Use the unit."

She climbed off his lap, hating to separate their bodies. Watching him scoot off the bed made her feel a little regret. Deviant naked was a great sight she wouldn't grow tired of appreciating.

"Do you know how to use a cleansing unit?"

"Yes. I traveled to the Colton Station on a luxury cruise ship, and they have nice ones aboard them."

"Those are expensive. At least from what I've heard."

"My sister paid. She is well off."

"What is her status on Earth?"

"She's a regular person, but she married a guy who owns his own company. He makes shuttle parts and she works with him. They do a lot of business."

"You really don't work for Earth Government as a spy, do you?" He intently studied her eyes.

"I don't." She hesitated and glanced up where he'd returned the knife. "Do you want proof? It hurts but…you could slice my leg to see the interior. It will heal in a few minutes as long as the cut is clean."

His eyes narrowed. "No. I could just borrow a scanner if I need proof of what you've said. I don't want you to suffer."

"Oh. Right. I didn't think of that."

He hesitated. "Go get clean. Take your time. I have to contact my father to tell him I've returned to my quarters. He wasn't outside the automated brothel when we left but I admit, I wasn't searching for him either. My priority was getting you to the ship."

She turned and stepped inside the cleansing unit. The door automatically sealed her inside as she studied the controls. They were standard, from Earth, and she turned it on. Foam began to spray and she closed her eyes, spread her limbs, and allowed the machine to do its job.

The foam melted into water, dripped off her body, and she checked her hair to make sure it had gotten clean. She inhaled and realized she now smelled a little like Deviant. He had some kind of scented body foam inside his unit. She turned and one of the shelves slid open, a towel revealed. She smiled. It was a nice unit, as good as the one on the cruiser.

She began to dry and her arm almost hit the door she'd entered through. It automatically slid open.

The room was empty, Deviant gone. She stared across the room at the door. A shiver ran down her spine but it had nothing to do with being chilled from the water still on her body. He'd said there were seven cyborgs on his ship, all men, and she worried over what would happen if someone found out she was hidden inside his room.

He'd made it clear he hadn't gotten permission to bring her aboard, since he'd said he was the only one who knew she were there. She would have to trust Deviant. Her luck with men had never been good, but so far he hadn't lied to her. Fear spread through her at the thought of what would happen if he did turn her over to his crew.

She dried her body quickly, her mind made up to try her best to keep the cyborg happy. It would hopefully make him less inclined to share her. She was a survivor, quick on her new feet, and at some point she needed to figure out where to go when she'd repaid her debt to Deviant. Staying with him in the meantime wouldn't be a hardship.

The wall of storage stumped her until she brushed her fingers over it and a drawer slid out. She hoped he wouldn't mind if she borrowed his stuff. She searched for clothes, not digging into his personal items until she found what appeared to be shirts. She took one off the top of the folded pile, pulled it down her body, and smiled at how it fell to mid-thigh. She rolled the sleeves to find her hands.

My cyborg is a pretty big guy.

She instantly chastised herself. "He's not mine," she muttered. "At least not for keeps."

She'd left Earth to live with her new husband, had hoped to find a happy life with the guy. Instead she'd ended up with a deceitful troll.

Deviant's smiling face flashed through her mind and longing hit. Why couldn't he have been the one who'd answered her ad?

Another idea struck and she chewed on her lip. Women from his planet didn't find him attractive. She'd overheard him say he had given up on having a family, but she wasn't blind. The idea of staying with him and possibly having little cyborgs wasn't an unpleasant thought. She'd always dreamed about having a few kids if she ever found the right man.

Maybe Deviant would decide to keep her. She really liked him, at least so far, and it could be the answer to both of them getting what they wanted. Of course, convincing him of that might take some time. And she had nothing but while she paid off her debt to the sexy cyborg. Perhaps he'd start to feel for her, the way she was already beginning to feel for him.

A hundred unanswered questions filled her mind but she tried to push them back. Why did the women cyborgs find Deviant unattractive? What kind of place did he call home?

She glanced around the room, hoping he didn't live on the ship most of his life. He'd mentioned a home world. That meant a planet that Earth wouldn't know about, so it had to be far from the solar system she'd been born in. Otherwise Earth would have tried to colonize it.

She made herself comfortable by dropping one of his pillows over her legs to keep them warm as she sat cross-legged on the bed. The plan of convincing Deviant to keep her for good played through her mind over and over. She liked it a lot. He could be an ass but she doubted it. They had time to get to know each other better.

Don't fall in love, she warned, afraid he might not return the feeling. That would be a bad scenario if she lost her heart to him, and he only saw her as a way to get some sexual experience.

58

She wasn't even certain he *could* fall in love. Did cyborgs feel those kinds of emotions?

* * * * *

Deviant stood in line with a tray. The crew had taken a break right before he'd entered the food services area and most of them seemed to be there. He linked with the onboard computer while he waited his turn, to leave a message for his father.

"I'm in my quarters. I need to privately speak to you when you return. Hail me but don't go there."

He cut the connection as the male in front of him walked away with his meal. He quickly filled one plate to capacity. The male behind him raised his eyebrows.

"Hungry?"

"It was too difficult to eat when I visited the station."

"The head coverings." Maze nodded. "I can relate."

He spun away and left before anyone else could question him about the amount of food he'd taken.

His father would smooth over the rules he'd broken by bringing Venice onboard the ship without permission. He knew it was procedure to contact the council first to get approval. She would have been located by the station owner before the council even answered, in that were the case. And more than likely, the council would have said no. Deviant wasn't willing to take that chance.

It was done now, Venice already aboard the cyborg shuttle, and he'd face whatever consequences were meted out to him as punishment. Venice had been a temptation he couldn't resist. A real female had asked for his help, offered herself to him, and they'd made a verbal agreement that she'd belong to him. It was a once-in-a-lifetime opportunity he refused to pass up.

She was on the small side, her skin tone pale enough to appear striking against his own. His logic could have been impaired by his physical urges. His pride hated to admit it but it didn't make it less true. His dick hardened just at the memory of her mouth wrapped around it. It had been the best feeling he'd ever experienced—right up until the moment she'd straddled his lap and he'd known how it felt to be inside a female.

A new lesson had been learned. Males not only joined family units to be a thriving part of their social community, or to breed and have a child they could help raise. It was to gain regular access to a female's body and the pleasures that came with it.

He paused outside his door to conceal his smile. He had his own female, one that no other males could enjoy. He wouldn't have to share Venice. She didn't want other males.

He accessed his room only after assuring the corridor was clear, to avoid her being seen. The door slid open with his access code. She sat on his bed with damp hair and a pillow over her lap. The smile she gave him only heightened the nice sensation at seeing her awaiting his arrival. He studied her expression closely, deciding the happiness was real. She was glad to see him.

"I brought you food."

"I'm starving. Thank you."

The reality of their situation slammed into his mind.

She was completely dependent upon him for everything. He had taken on a role he'd never considered before. She'd need clothing, food, and protection.

Pride was an emotion he rarely experienced, but it flooded him as he sat on the bed next to her. She was truly his.

"You eat first."

"We can share." She smiled again, her gaze holding his. "Do you want me to feed you?"

He wasn't sure what that meant and admitted as much.

She glanced down, took hold of a utensil, and stabbed a cut piece of meat protein. He tensed when she lifted it toward his face, wondering if she'd attack. She could be working for Earth Government after all.

The fork paused in front of his lips. "Open up."

No deceit registered in her eyes to him. He parted his mouth and was stunned when she gently eased the bite inside. He took it as she withdrew the potential weapon. He chewed, watching her closely as she took her own bite. She stabbed another protein and offered it to him again.

"See? It's kind of nice, isn't it?"

He gave a nod, chewing while studying her features. They were delicate, and he couldn't detect any scars. Curiosity became stronger as he allowed her to feed him the meal, Venice taking bites between the ones she gave him. All the questions he had about her waited until the food was gone. She set the tray aside and sipped from the same cup as him.

Sharing was a nice thing, he decided, having never experienced it on such a personal level before.

"What kind of accident did you have on Earth that damaged you?"

She passed over the cup to him. "The car's computer experienced some kind of failure or glitch while I was traveling home from work. It happened so fast, I didn't have time to override the system before the vehicle careened to the left. I struck the divider wall and it flipped over." Her expression flashed sadness, if he read her right. "It's kind of a blur after that point. I was in a lot of pain and trapped in the wreckage. It caught fire, and I remember thinking it was over for me, you know? That's how I got burned. Emergency drones arrived to put it out thankfully, cut me from the wreckage, and then a medical transport took me away. I knew I was pretty messed up. I kept passing out...and there was so much blood."

"You said they took your blood? Why? They can manufacture it on Earth. It would normally be a higher-quality product than the real thing."

"Rich people like the best, and to them, it seems that means the real stuff."

Her mouth firmed into a tight line as she paused speaking. That was anger. He liked that he could identify her emotions, and that she didn't hide them from him.

"I kept hoping I'd wake to see my sister at my bedside, but they kept me drugged most of the time. I'd come around sometimes, and then an android nurse would enter the cubical, refuse to answer my questions, and drug me again. It was shocking to find out just how long they'd had me there after I was freed."

"You were unconscious most of the time?"

"Yes. I'd probably be insane otherwise. I can't image being strapped to a bed for those years, fully conscious but unable to get free, knowing they were keeping me alive just to take my blood."

"Was it painful when the drugs wore off?"

"I was able to lift my head a few times." Tears gathered in her eyes but she blinked rapidly to be rid of them. "I saw how messed up I was. It's kind of hard to miss it when you try to brush your hair back from your face and only one arm responds. The other one was gone. It felt like my legs were still there, but they wouldn't move when I tried to struggle out of the straps they had across my body. It was another big shock when I first realized they were gone too."

The urge to pull her into his arms overcame Deviant, and he only hesitated for a moment before he reached out and took her hand. It was the artificial one. He wouldn't have known by touch if she hadn't told him. She clung to him, seeming to welcome the gesture.

"It must have been traumatic." He couldn't imagine what she'd endured. To be helpless was a fear of his. He didn't verbally express it.

"I was sure I'd die in there...but then I woke to see two people hovering above me. I thought it was a dream when they unstrapped me and lifted me onto a gurney. They had hacked into the mainframe and shut down the androids that ran the facility. They pushed me right past them and told me they were taking me to my sister."

"You have a strong attachment to her." It wasn't a question. He could hear it in her voice when it softened.

"We were always close. It was tough to leave her behind but I didn't have a choice. I had to flee Earth before I was found. Not only would I have been killed or returned to that horrible place, but she would have been punished. My being alive would just be proof that she had a part in my escape. That would have been a death sentence for her. They call that treason, when you do anything against Earth Government."

"I am sorry for your loss. Perhaps you could contact her at a later date."

"No. It's too dangerous. We said our goodbyes when I left. I'm safe from Earth Government right now but she still lives there. They'll be watching her too closely. I'm sure they have to be worried about what happened to me, and if I'll somehow get my story out to the general population."

She sighed, her thumb rubbing against his finger where they were clasped together. "Not that it would do any good, even if my story outraged anyone. The people in charge would just kill any protestors or make them disappear. Everyone is too afraid to stand up against Earth Government, no matter how corrupt they've become."

"I don't have a flattering opinion of Earth, either."

Chapter Four

Venice held Deviant's gaze as he watched her. "What is the real story behind cyborgs leaving Earth?"

"What were you told?"

"There was some kind of chip malfunction that made them…" She paused. "That made your kind unstable and kind of, um, homicidal. I remember hearing that cyborgs killed a lot of people."

"That isn't entirely correct. We became self-aware and demanded to be given rights instead of being subjected to slavery. We might be constructed by cloned material, but we're sentient beings with our own thoughts and feelings. Earth Government treated us as if we were only fleshy androids. They deemed us a failure and ordered us destroyed. They felt we were flawed. We rebelled and fled the planet to survive. The only deaths that resulted were when we attempted to defend ourselves against being murdered."

"They really are assholes. I take it the rumors that you guys are out in deep space attacking shuttles to get spare body parts isn't true, either?" She laughed. It was a pleasant sound to him. "I noticed you're all one color and not a patchwork of other people."

He smiled, amused. "No. Manufactured limbs are much better if there is a need for a replacement."

"There's no need to tell *me*." She glanced down her body at her arm and legs. "My authentic parts can't heal fast the way these babies can." She looked up and shrugged. "They're also stronger and more reliable. My artificial limbs never fall asleep if I stay in one position for too long and I never have to shave my legs again."

He glanced down. "They are beautiful."

"Thank you."

"They appear real."

"They feel like it. I can't tell the difference most of the time."

Deviant wanted her again. "Lay back and spread them apart for me."

She didn't hesitate, and he liked that she followed his orders without protest. It was sexy when she eased back and he shoved up the shirt, exposing her sex and lower stomach. She parted her legs, bending them up so he could scoot closer. He studied her legs, his fingers tracing the pale skin. There were no flaws or indications of where her true skin ended and the artificial legs began. He leaned down and studied her sex. He used his thumb and forefinger to spread the lips and get a better look.

"I could look at you all day," he announced. He lifted his gaze and liked the way her features appeared flushed. Her cheeks were pink and her eyelids narrowed slightly. He also detected her breathing rate had increased.

"Talk me through what you like."

"Oral sex?"

"Yes." He licked his lips to wet them and noticed the way she sucked in a deep breath.

"You want to spread me wide open so you have room to put your mouth down there. See my clit?"

He glanced down. "Yes."

"That's where you want to focus. There's a little hood area and you want to touch just under there. It's the most sensitive spot." She smoothed her hands down and gripped her legs under her bent knees, spreading her legs wider. "You know how you kiss me? Try it there."

It was a fascinating concept. Cyborg females in family units demanded males give them oral sex, and it was a skill he'd need if one ever offered to contract with him. Though he found he suddenly didn't care so much about that as he lowered farther, twisting his body to lay flat on his stomach. It put his face between her thighs. Right now, he just wanted Venice, wanted to please her.

She smelled good to him and he opened his mouth, hesitant in case he somehow hurt her. She looked so delicate there. He glanced up and discovered that she watched him.

"You don't have to do this." Her breathing had increased.

"I want to. Just tell me if I do it wrong."

He inched closer and allowed his tongue to test against her clit. She tensed and he licked again, learning the feel of the tender flesh. Deviant liked the way she softly moaned, urging him to continue to explore and test how she reacted. He remembered her comment about kissing so he pressed his lips around the nub of her sex and swirled his tongue across it. He liked the way she tasted.

"Oh yeah," she moaned, urging him on.

He remembered how it felt when Venice had her mouth wrapped around him and became more aggressive, since it didn't seem to hurt her. Her sounds of pleasure increased and she wiggled her hips, almost pulling away from his tongue. He shifted his hold on her and pinned her hips down.

His dick throbbed at the sounds of her fractured gasps and moans. He sucked a little as he licked and he was amazed that the pink, fleshy bulb stiffened as he played with it. It was almost as if she hardened the way he did when he was aroused. He continued to suck and lick at her until she cried out loudly, and he could feel her twitch against his tongue as she climaxed. The nub he'd played with eventually softened.

He pulled back a little and looked down. Her slit was soaked, the smell of her arousal stronger and even more appealing.

Venice panted and she released her legs. "That was amazing. You're good at it."

He rose and reached down, tearing open his pants. He freed his thick shaft and climbed up her. Venice didn't object as he pinned her under him and gently entered her. Sheer pleasure gripped him as tightly as her wet, hot pussy did. It was the best feeling, to be inside her body.

"Look at me," he demanded.

Venice stared at him, and he started to move in deep, slow thrusts. She moaned and reached up, wrapping her arms around his neck. He wished the shirt weren't on her, wanting to feel her bare skin against his. He just wasn't willing to withdraw from her body and strip them both. The urge to fuck her was too strong to be denied.

He bent his legs, braced them, and pumped harder. The bed shook but no pain or fear showed in her features. She moaned and wrapped her legs around his waist in response.

He moved faster and the pleasure increased. A beep sounded in the background but he ignored it, not caring about anything but finding his own release—which came with brutal force. He clenched his teeth to avoid making loud noises. The strong aftermath left him trembling when he stilled on top of Venice.

Her hands stroked his back and her grip around his hips lessened. "I love feeling you inside me," she admitted.

Deviant realized she hadn't climaxed with him, and he tensed. "I'm sorry."

"For what?" Her gaze wasn't accusing or angry.

"You felt too good and I was selfish."

She smiled. "You got me off first. That just amplified it when you were inside me. I have no complaints."

The beep sounded again and she turned her gaze toward the door. Someone was in the hallway, wanting admittance. Venice looked afraid, and Deviant lifted his head.

"It will be my father. No one else visits me. I left him a message to contact me but not to come to my quarters." He regretted having to pull out of her. He liked being buried inside her body, connected to her on such an intimate level. "Go use the cleansing unit. I've sweat on you. I'll let you know when it's safe to come out."

She moved fast for a human. He hated the fear that drove her to reach the cleaning unit quickly. He shouldn't have told her there were seven males onboard but her being safe had been his priority. He stood and closed his pants. He touched the pad to be certain it was his father.

"Yes?"

"Were you in the cleansing unit? I was about to override the lock to enter."

He opened the door and stared at his father. "Come in."

The elder cyborg stepped inside and Deviant sealed the doors just in case Venice didn't wait for him to tell her it was safe. He turned, facing his grim-featured parent.

"You were always advanced with your learning skills but I gave you twelve hours for a reason, Deviant. Why don't you return to the station until the end of the current shift? Our females are harsh critics. Passable skills won't do. Most of them enjoy timed, short intercourse but I've heard some like to test a male on endurance. You need to learn to hold your seed until they say you can release. The sex bots will help you learn that skill, but you need to spend more time with them to do that. You're naturally born, without the same implants I have. It means you're unable to control your body functions as well as I can."

The slight hum of the cleansing unit being turned on sounded. Mavo, his father, startled and glanced at it. "Is it malfunctioning?"

"It's in use." Deviant held his father's confused stare. "I need your help."

"You stole a sex bot?"

"No."

Mavo glanced at the unit, then back at Deviant. "I don't understand."

"She's an Earther."

Deviant anticipated his father would be surprised, but he hadn't expected the male to stumble back a step. "What?"

"She's being hunted. We made an deal. I am taking her with me and keeping her safe. In exchange, she has agreed to belong to me."

"Hunted by whom?"

"The station owner. He contracted her to leave Earth to be his bride. She was hiding inside the brothel and approached me."

"You helped the wife escape from him? Onto our *ship*?" Mavo paled.

"The marriage contract isn't valid. He lured her into deep space with the illegal marriage contract to gain a forced sex worker."

"You helped a slave escape?"

Deviant gave a slight nod. "I need your help smoothing things over. She is my property. I didn't have time to contact the council to ask for permission and I doubt they would have given it. I know that was wrong, but I made the decision, regardless."

"They wouldn't have permitted you to take her." Mavo seemed to get his surprise under control and blew out a deep breath. "She agreed to be your property? We don't own Earthers on Garden anymore."

"She's agreed to be mine, with conditions. I don't care *what* the council wants to call it but we have a verbal contract that she belongs to me."

"What are the conditions?"

"No other males are permitted to touch her. I agreed."

His father blinked a few times. "*Other* males... You are allowed to touch her?"

Deviant glanced at the bed. It was mussed from what they'd just done on it and one pillow had fallen on the floor. The other one had moved and white, feminine panties were in plain view. His father followed his stare then glanced back at him, watching him evaluate the scene.

His dad jerked his head back, openly gazing at him with amusement.

"I see. So I sent you to have sex with a sex bot and instead you brought back a real female. I don't know if I should be impressed or outraged."

"She needed my help, and our exchange is a good one."

"I would say so." Mavo stepped closer and lowered his voice. "Are you certain she's not from Earth Government?"

"She's not."

"You took precautions?"

"I've secured the room. She can't leave or send signals. But I believe her. She's been modified enough that Earth doesn't consider her a human being anymore."

"She's been turned into a cyborg?"

"No. She's been given three artificial limbs and some internal work."

Mavo frowned.

"Both of her legs and one arm were damaged in an accident, so she has replacements, along with a few internal organs and bones. Her limbs appear very real. The work was excellent and high grade. I couldn't tell they were replaced." He quickly relayed what he'd learned. "Earth Government would destroy her or return her to a medical prison to harvest her rare blood type." He went on to explain a little more.

Mavo nodded. "We have to verify her information."

"I'm willing to allow you to have her scanned."

"This isn't going to be easy to justify to the council."

"She's mine. She'll state to the council that she's contracted to me, if they wish to ask."

Mavo frowned, studying him closely. "Do you see her as someone contracted to you as property, or are you using that term to sway me into helping you?"

"She's an individual, but her wish to be with me is relevant." Deviant tensed, watching his father. He needed his support. "I'm unique," he argued. "Other females haven't wanted me. Venice does. She doesn't see me as flawed."

A flash of pain showed in his father's eyes before he concealed it. "I'd like to meet her."

"Give me a few minutes. I need to explain the situation to her."

Mavo walked to the door. "I'll wait outside."

"Make sure the hallway is clear before you reenter."

"Of course. The last thing we need is other males knowing there is a female from Earth onboard. Some would worry she's a spy. Others would vie for her attention."

"None will get near her," Deviant swore.

Deviant opened and closed the door to allow his father to leave, then walked over to the cleansing unit to override the controls. It opened, and he took a moment to appreciate the sight of Venice with foam melting off her nude body.

She smiled, not angry at his interruption.

"My father is waiting in the hallway and he wishes to meet you."

She stopped the spray and began to dry. "Okay."

"He'll help us smooth over my bringing you to our home world."

"What's the worst that could happen?"

He detected worry in her expression. "You need to tell anyone who asks that you've verbally contracted to belong to me." He reached out and brushed his thumb along her cheek. "You're more than that to me, but we have laws in place that would allow me to keep you safe if you were considered indentured."

"Would they kill me or something otherwise?"

"No but you wouldn't be trusted. We are very suspicious of anyone from Earth, because the fate of our world rests on them not being able to locate our planet. Your government would attempt to destroy us again."

"They aren't mine anymore. So...my being your property makes me less of a threat to other cyborgs?"

"Belonging to me protects you from being interrogated or held as a prisoner. With my protection extended to you, I would take full responsibility for all of your actions."

She peered at him with a frown. "You mean *you'd* be punished if I did something wrong? That doesn't sound fair."

"They couldn't detain you without my permission, which I would never give."

That answer didn't seem to put her at ease but she nodded. "Okay. I got it."

He turned away and walked to the wall, opening a panel. He withdrew one of his shirts and some sleeping pants. He sliced a foot of material off the bottom of the legs before handing the outfit to her. "Put this on."

She dressed quickly and Deviant resisted smiling. His clothing was far too large for her, even with the shortened pants.

She brushed her hands down the material and held his gaze. "How do I look?"

"Very attractive."

"I wish I had something better to wear to meet your dad. He's going to think I'm a refugee...which I guess I am. I had to leave all my belongings on the station."

"We'll get you suitable clothing once we reach Garden."

"That's the name of your planet?"

"Yes. My father waits. Are you ready? His name is Mavo."

She gave a sharp nod but he glimpsed a little fear in her expression.

"No one would dare do you harm, Venice. I'd defend you against anyone—and that includes my father. You're mine to protect."

75

Venice felt a little stunned at the vehemence of Deviant's promise. It did alleviate some of her nervousness though. He touched the pad for seconds and it opened. A tall black-haired cyborg entered. His green eyes were piercing as they studied her from head to foot. The door closed behind him and he paused just inside.

"Father, this is Venice." Deviant stepped to her side and gently curved his arm around her waist. "This is my father, Mavo."

She smiled. "Hello. It's nice to meet you." She held out her hand, hoping the gesture wouldn't offend him.

He stepped forward and took her offered palm, grasping it gently and shaking it twice. He didn't release it though. Instead, he looked down and frowned. "Real or artificial?"

She remembered his voice from the brothel. Now he just wasn't dressed like a pirate. "Real. My left one is artificial, and both of my legs."

"May I?" He released her hand.

She offered him the left one. He took it, studying her fingers. "Amazing. Earth has really advanced medically since we left. It feels genuine."

"It does. I can't tell a difference from my right or left unless I get cut. It hurts but I don't bleed on the left side. It heals really fast too."

Venice studied Mavo. He looked too young to be Deviant's father. She could see a resemblance though with his facial features. They had the same chin, lips, and nose. The eye colors were different and so were their skin tones. Mavo was a much lighter shade of gray. His green eyes were pretty but she preferred Deviant's brilliant blue ones. The cyborg released her hand.

"Convince me you don't work for Earth Government."

Deviant answered before she could. "We discussed this, Father. Scan her body and check Earth laws. I believe her."

Mavo frowned, switching his attention to his son. "You're motivated to believe her. I'm worried about your safety, and that of our people."

"I will take responsibility for her."

"And if she is a spy?" Mavo sighed. "It could cost you your life, along with risking our entire planet. We don't want to go to war with Earth."

"Earth Government will kill me or put me back into the facility where they were stealing and selling my blood, if they ever get their hands on me," Venice informed him. "They kept me there for four years, drugged up, and under the care of androids. Do you think I ever want to go back there? One full scan and they'll know who I am and what was done to me. All this body work is illegal. I'm not a person anymore, according to Earth laws. They can order me destroyed like I'm some kind of outdated piece of machinery someone patched together out of spare parts.

"I can't ever go back, nor do I want to. I'm also terrified of what they'll do to my sister. She was the one who kept searching for me, despite being told I'd died. They'll kill her if EG is ever given evidence that I'm alive, because it will be proof against her that she helped me escape. That would be considered a terminal crime."

"Won't she be blamed anyway?"

"No. They're probably suspicious of her but as long as I don't turn up alive, the blame could shift to rebels who attack those kinds of facilities to make them lose profits. Rebels would have killed me and disposed of my body, just so my blood couldn't be sold any longer. Only a family member would bother paying for extensive surgery to get me back on my feet."

He continued to stare at her with a frown.

"She paid an organization called Angels to help retrieve me. They're on government hit lists, considered a terrorist group, like the rebels are. The difference is, most of their members are medical professionals who are tired of seeing people like me killed or used until death. They patched me up this great because my sister donated a lot of money to them. That would be seen as her funding a terrorist group. Do you understand? It's a death sentence for her."

Mavo studied her and finally relaxed. "I want to believe you. Right now, I need to contact the council and inform them, along with the commander of this vessel, that someone from Earth is aboard."

"Perhaps we should wait until after we reach Garden." Deviant lowered his voice. "I don't want anyone believing they can take her away from me."

"They won't." Mavo held Venice's gaze. "We used to be able to own Earthers, but now we can't. We can, however, contract them as workers, taking them under our protection. I have a few friends on the council. I'll contact them directly first, then let Stag know."

"He doesn't like Earthers." Deviant softened his tone too. "I'd really prefer we wait until we reach Garden. Think about it for a moment."

Mavo hesitated. "I'll make certain you're off duty until we return, so you don't have to leave her alone. Let me know when you need food. I'll bring it so you don't have to risk anyone finding out she's here. I still need to let a few council members that I trust know what is happening. You won't be able to get her off this shuttle and into the city otherwise."

"Understood. Thank you."

"We are undocking with the station in a few hours. I'll talk to you in the morning. It will be too late by then to change your mind about taking her home with you."

"My decision is made," Deviant stated.

Venice watched Deviant's father leave before voicing her concerns. "Who is Stag and why does he hate anyone from Earth?"

"He was heavily abused while on Earth. This is his ship we're aboard."

She suddenly didn't feel very safe. "Would this Stag have me tossed out an airlock or something if he finds out I'm aboard? I've heard that some captains do that when they discover a stowaway."

"No. That sounds like something only Earthers would do. I won't allow anyone to hurt you, Venice. I would fight Stag before I'd let him near you." He reached out and brushed his hand down her arm. "That's why I explained how important it is for you to stay here, so no one finds out about you."

"I thought the scariest part was knowing I was the only woman with seven men on the ship. Now I'm more afraid of the guy with a grudge."

He smiled. "You're mine, Venice. I will protect you. We'll reach Garden and everything will be fine."

She wanted to trust him. It sure beat still being on the station with Darbis hunting her down, trying to force her to work in a brothel.

She really liked Deviant, and was starting to care about him more than she should. Her heart might get broken in the end if she didn't rein in her feelings. It was just tough not to be attracted to him on every level. She reminded herself that one day he wanted to join in some family unit thing with a female cyborg.

"Can I ask you something?"

"Anything." He led her to the bed and sat.

She took the seat next to him. "What's wrong with cyborg women?"

He arched his eyebrows in question.

"I still can't understand why you'd have a problem dating them."

Deviant hesitated and then blew out a deep breath. "My mother had a difficult time conceiving me. I wasn't her first child, but I was her last. She already had four sons but it was decided I'd be her fifth."

"That's a lot of kids."

"She had one son from each of her other three husbands and two with my father. He was her fourth."

"She was married four times?"

He reached out and took her hand. "She has four current husbands."

Venice was stunned. She'd heard of some weird family relationships on Earth. Sometimes the rich would keep a spouse and a known lover, but it was rare for it to become public knowledge.

"The cyborg males vastly outnumbered the females when we fled Earth. It was logical to have them take as many males as possible into a family unit to avoid fighting."

She was confused, and it must have shown because he shrugged.

"I know it's not the way it is on Earth. We had to adapt. The males might have started to fight amongst themselves, killing off the competition to win a female's attention, and we needed to make certain our race survived. Some females have more than four husbands, but four is the standard number."

"More?"

"Some keep six or seven. I have even met one male who was the eighth. It depends on how fertile the female is and how many males she's willing to accept. Each of us must produce a child to ensure the future of our race."

He was a virgin, or had been before they'd met. She refrained from asking him if he had any kids since that seemed highly improbable. "Okay. I guess I can see how that could happen if there are so few women and a lot of men. Don't the husbands get jealous and still fight?"

"They don't live together. The females split their time between the males in their family units. The women move between the homes the males keep, taking their children with them. Jealousy isn't a factor that arises much."

"That's hard to believe." Venice tried to relate by imagining having to share Deviant with another woman or a group of them. She didn't like the thought one bit.

"It's difficult to explain."

That was an understatement. "So in other words, there are so many men that it's tough to find a woman who doesn't already have a ton of husbands?"

"We located more cyborg females recently, so the numbers aren't as uneven as they used to be. My mother had to take experimental drugs to produce me. I told you that she had two children with my father. Dalk was born first, and showed exceptional intelligence at a young age. My mother stripped my father of the right to raise him by giving him to another male as his son."

"That sounds really messed up! She was allowed to do that?"

He inclined his head. "It was. She has a strong bond to her first husband. Their child was born with flaws. Perfection is desired with cyborg parents, a source of pride, so she allowed him to claim Dalk as his own so he'd have a healthy son. My father was stripped of the right to raise and be a part of Dalk's life. He protested, but she ignored his wishes. So my father took my mother before the council, and they ordered her to have another child that he could retain established rights to. He had also promised to have a child for his friend Krell, who wasn't able to meet his requirement to produce a child for our society."

Venice opened her mouth, found no words since she was so confused, and ended up just sealing her lips. His world sounded pretty complicated.

"Krell is heavily scarred and no female wanted to join in a family unit with him. He and my father are close friends, and have been since they fled Earth together. I'm legally registered to Krell, to fulfill his obligation to our race. But as I stated, my mother had a difficult time getting pregnant. Or perhaps she was angry enough over the council's ruling that she attempted not to have another child. The experimental drug the council ordered her to take to conceive had unexpected results." He released her and fisted his hand. "My skin tone is much darker than that of any other cyborg."

"So?" Venice glanced at his hand, then back to his face. "There's nothing wrong with that."

His gaze and expression softened. "I am glad you believe so, but flaws in our society are an embarrassment to parents and to our race. Most children born with defects are able to overcome them with surgeries. That's not possible with me. They attempted to treat my skin when I was younger with pigmentation therapy but it only darkened it more."

Anger stirred fast inside her. "That's bullshit. There's nothing wrong with your skin!"

"My eyes are another flaw."

She peered into them, shocked. "They're gorgeous."

"They hold a luminosity factor that wasn't expected."

"They're very bright but they're breathtaking."

"Thank you." He took her hand again, lacing his fingers through hers. "Some cyborg females are uncomfortable looking at me. They don't want my flaws passed down to their children, and it's probable those traits are hereditary. They banned the drug to make certain no others were born like me."

She let that sink in. "So that's why you're not married? Women on your planet are dumb and superficial?"

He chuckled. "Yes."

"Their loss in my gain." She leaned in closer and reached up with her free hand to press her palm against his chest. "You're the best-looking man I've ever seen."

The pained look that flashed across his face, and the way he studied her as if he wasn't sure she was being honest, about broke her heart. She released his hand and stood, straddling his lap.

"I mean it, Deviant. I get turned-on just looking at you. You're perfect. Don't let anyone ever tell you otherwise. Believe me." She trailed her hand up his chest to his shoulder and leaned in. "Do you think I'm flawed because three of my limbs are add-ons?"

He shook his head. "No."

"Would they think that on your world?"

"Possibly."

"Then fuck them. All that matters is what *we* think—and guess what? I want you...and I hope you want me."

He wrapped his arms around her waist. "You're perfect to me too, Venice. I want you as well."

She smiled. "We're on a bed. Isn't that convenient?"

He smiled back. "I like the way you think."

"I like the way you do everything."

Chapter Five

Venice woke and stretched, the firm, warm body behind her causing her to smile. She rolled over, facing Deviant, who slept on his side. Memories of the evening before almost had her chuckling.

The handsome cyborg had let her ride him once they'd shed their clothing, but then he'd tried to get dressed again to go to sleep. She'd refused to let him.

It had stunned him a bit to consider sleeping nude with her, but she'd shown him the advantages by roaming her hands all over his chest and lower. That had turned into another bout of sex. He was a fast learner. Deviant might kill her if he got any better at making her have multiple orgasms.

"Hey," she whispered. The lighting was dim in the room but she knew the moment his eyes opened. They literally glowed a bit. They were beautiful.

"Hi." He blinked a few times. "How did you sleep?"

"Really well." She loved his eyes, couldn't stop staring into them.

His smile faded. "Computer, increase lights by ten percent."

The blue of his eyes were still bright but the glowing ceased as the room grew brighter. "Why did you do that?"

"I forgot what happens in dim lighting."

"Your eyes are beautiful, Deviant. Computer? Dim the lights by ten percent."

Nothing happened.

Deviant sighed. "Computer, dim lights by ten percent." It complied. "Sorry. I had to lock voice commands as a precaution. I trust you but it alleviated my father's worry that you'd attempt to contact Earth."

She understood, peering at his eyes again. "They really *are* beautiful. You don't have to hide anything from me."

He grinned. "In that case..." He shifted his body closer, his stiff cock brushing against her belly. "I want you again."

"Making up for lost time? I have no objections." She reached under the covers, wrapping her fingers gently around his shaft and stroking his erect flesh. "That's the best way to start a morning."

A bell chimed.

"That would be my father." He rolled away from her with a sigh, shoved off the covers and stood. "Go into the cleansing unit and take these to put on." He crossed the room, opening up a drawer. He tossed her a shirt and shorts, removing a pair of pants for himself.

Venice hurried out of bed and took the clothing with her. She placed them high on a shelf and turned on the unit, first activated the toilet to come out for use, then cleaning her body and brushing her teeth at the same time.

She wondered if Deviant's father had contacted his council friends and if things were about to turn bad. What if Deviant was ordered to return her to Darbis's station? It was a grim, terrifying thought. She hurried to finish the cycle and dry off, putting on the borrowed clothing.

Deviant and his father both turned when she stepped out. She forced a smile she didn't feel and nodded to Mavo. A tray of food rested on top of the bed. She was hungry but resisted investigating what he'd brought.

"Father has contacted his friend Krell to explain the situation. A few of the council members owe him favors. They are going to smooth things over for you to live on Garden with me."

That sounded like good news to Venice. "So everything is going to be fine?"

"Yes." Mavo glanced up and down her body. "They will want to medically scan you. It won't be painful. I apologize, but my race isn't trusting of Earthers. I hope you can understand."

"I do. I'd be leery of telling anyone associated with Earth Government my secrets, too. They'd put a price on my head and I'd have bounty hunters looking for me to take me back."

"That will never happen." Deviant inched closer to her. "You're safe now."

She liked how protective he was. "I believe that. Thank you."

"Krell agrees with your assessment, Deviant, and believes Stag will become a problem. We have decided to keep him unaware of her presence on the *Varnish*. You have a shift in less than an hour. We must resume normal duties to prevent suspicion." Mavo glanced at Venice, then his son. "I take third shift. I thought I could keep her company so she's not left

87

alone. I'll have just enough time to wait for you to return before I go on duty."

"She won't betray my trust." Deviant scowled.

"It's possible they could detect her presence. I'd rather one of us be with her at all times in case of that event. She'd be alone otherwise, and have no way to defend herself if security investigated."

"The odds of that happening are slim. We don't perform life scans ship-wide as part of standard operations."

"We've had some issues with the oxygen scrubbers in section four. They could have to reset life support or test carbon monoxide levels. What is the procedure?"

Deviant grunted. "They would scan to see who's in the surrounding areas and make them aware of the issue."

Mavo inclined his head. "They would detect her. I'll stay."

Venice got an uneasy feeling but Deviant turned to her. "You'll be safe with my father. I must go on shift or someone will come see why I am not on duty. A medic would arrive first, security next."

"Okay." She glanced at the other cyborg. The last thing she wanted was to be left alone with him but she understood why Deviant needed to leave.

"My father won't harm you. He's contracted with my mother in a family unit."

Venice gave him a questioning look.

Deviant opened his mouth but it was Mavo who spoke first.

"I'm not interested in having sex with you. My son shared the terms of your agreement. I just plan to keep you company while he's not here, for your safety."

That was certainly clear enough. "Okay."

Deviant sighed. "I need to get ready. Eat."

He grabbed a uniform out of one of the storage bins in the wall and entered the cleansing unit. Venice regarded Mavo. "Well, at least we'll get to know each other."

He nodded. "I'd like that. Do eat. Don't allow my presence to hinder you from what you would normally do."

She turned and moved the tray to the floor, quickly making the bed. She replaced the tray and sat on one corner. "Would you like to sit? There are no chairs in here."

He crossed the room to the other side of the long sleeping bunk and sat. She hesitated briefly but started to eat. The cleansing unit made soft noises as Deviant showered. Venice was hungry but she picked at her food.

"What do you think of cyborgs?"

She swallowed and turned her head, meeting his curious gaze. "I'm not sure how to answer that."

"Do we frighten you?"

"I don't know much about your kind but I'm not afraid of Deviant," she admitted.

"Have you heard that we kill Earthers to steal their flesh?"

"I have but I don't buy it, now that I've seen so much of your son."

She instantly regretted admitting that but taking the words back weren't an option.

She blushed a little and went on. "Deviant explained why you guys really left Earth. I believe his version of the story. Earth Government lies all the time and tries to use fear to control the population. That's probably why they spread word that cyborgs were deadly threats, to make certain no one sympathized with your plight."

"Tell me about this station owner you are married to."

She grimaced. "It was a scam. The man I spoke to on communications was just an employee, not the real man. I mean, he wasn't Darbis Martin. They did a bait and switch."

"What is that? I'm not familiar with that term."

"They advertise one thing, but then you get something totally different. It's never a good thing. I came out into deep space believing he wanted a wife, but instead, when I got there, they were going to force me to work in a brothel. He bragged about marrying a lot of previous women to get them to his station. The marriage isn't legal." She shuddered at the thought. "I managed to escape before they could take me to the brothel. That's not what I signed on for."

"I understand."

"Your son rescued me. I'm trying to put myself in your shoes, and I just want to assure you that I'd never do anything to hurt Deviant. I heard you say he would be punished if I were a spy. I'm not. I die if I'm recaptured."

"You don't mind being my son's property? Earthers hate that term."

"I hate to break it to you, but nobody is free."

"Explain."

"Earth Government tells us where we can live, what kind of jobs we can have, and they decide who can live or die. That was a government-run facility where I was kept prisoner. It wouldn't even shock me if I were to learn they'd rigged my vehicle to crash." It was something she'd contemplated. "They keep track of everything we do, and of every detailed medical scan. For all I know, they did this to me on purpose because of my rare blood type. They thought nothing of stealing my life away from me. With Deviant, I made a *choice*. I offered to belong to him. See the difference? I do. And no, I don't mind. He's a good man."

"You're wise."

"I wouldn't go that far. I agreed to be a deep-space bride out of desperation and it landed me on that station. Deviant saved me from a fate worse than death."

"You believe death is better than being a sex worker? You made an agreement to have sex with my son. What is the difference?"

"The difference is I'm attracted to Deviant."

He frowned.

"What? You find that hard to believe?"

"Our women only see his flaws."

That pissed her off all over again. "He's not flawed. What in the hell is wrong with your people? So his skin is darker than yours? So what? Mine is very pale. It's just skin. People should be judged by what's inside instead, and he's an amazing person. As for his eyes, they glow. So what? I think they're the prettiest eyes I've ever seen."

91

A smile curved Mavo's lips. "You don't see him as defective."

"No. I don't."

"Good. I don't see him that way either. He is a good man. He has honor and heart."

"I know. He saved me from hell. I'm never going to forget that or stop being grateful."

"I'm certain the station owner would have kept you alive."

"For a while, until I grew sick. A lot of his clients are pirates. We all know what that means."

"I don't."

"Pirates suffer from long-term exposure to radiation. I'm sure you've seen them. The sores. The disfigurements. About ten years ago, a group of women were rescued in deep space. They'd been captured by pirates months before." Venice abandoned her food, hugging her chest. "They'd been turned into breeders." She held his gaze. "It was all over the news. Earth Government wanted to use them as an example of why you don't leave the safe zones in space, which the military patrols. The women had been repeatedly raped by pirates...they suffered grave injuries because of the secondary radiation exposure through sexual contact. Do I need to go on?"

He shook his head. "No."

She nodded. "That would have been me. The reports kept everyone updated on their deteriorating conditions. I think the longest one survived for almost two years. She'd lost her hair, and her teeth had fallen out...you get the point. I doubt they were given treatment, just so EC could really scare the hell out of the public by showing vids of those poor women. I didn't see any high-tech medical facility at the Colton Station. Darbis would have used me to make money until my body gave out. Tell me that's not worse than death."

The cleansing unit opened and Deviant stepped out fully dressed. He put on his boots and studied her and his father. "Are you two on good terms?"

"We are," Mavo answered. "Start your shift.

Deviant hesitated, staring directly at her.

She rose and approached him. "It's okay. Your father is being very nice to me. I feel safe. Go do what you do. I'll be here waiting for you when you come back."

He reached out and gently brushed his thumb down her arm. "I'll be thinking of you."

That made her smile. "I'll be thinking about you too. You didn't eat," she reminded him.

"I will on my way to my shift. You eat what my father brought." He dropped his hand and spun, marching to the door. He hesitated then glanced back. Mavo stood and moved between them.

"Go. I'm blocking her if there's someone in the corridor."

Deviant left and the door sealed behind him. Venice felt a moment of uncertainty being left alone with his father but the cyborg turned around, holding her gaze.

"You should finish all the food. I need to make some reports and monitor the ship's internal communications while they do repairs on life support. I want to know immediately if they are made aware of your presence. Just go about whatever you would normally do." He walked to the door and placed his hand on the panel next to it, closing his eyes.

Venice took a seat on the bed and finished eating. It was strange having Mavo just standing there. He kind of reminded her of a breathing statue. A hundred questions filled her mind.

It seemed as if an hour had passed before he opened his eyes and stopped touching the panel. "The life support is fully restored. They aren't expecting any more issues with it. This is good news."

"You got all that from your hand touching the wall?"

"Yes. Did my son tell you about our cybernetics?"

"We didn't really discuss that."

"We were created the way clones were but they added chips and technology into our bodies so we could perform certain functions." He drew closer and showed her his hand. "I have sensors under my palms that send information directly to the chips implanted inside my brain. We can connect to computers by touch."

"That's handy." She smiled.

He didn't smile back.

"That was a joke. Get it? Handy? It's in your hand."

"Ah. A pun. I like your humor."

"You didn't think it was funny."

"I appreciate that you would try. My mood isn't the best today."

"Because of me?"

"Things have just been stressful lately. I don't want to discuss it. No offense."

She didn't pry, returning to their original topic. "So Deviant can do that too? Touch the panel and connect to the computer?"

"Yes. He was born instead of grown inside a vat, but the technology is easily copied to pass down to our children. He was implanted at the age of two. We discovered the younger the age, the easier they adapt to the technology."

She frowned.

"You have an issue with that?"

"That sounds so young."

"I was created on Earth in a factory. I never had parents. Deviant was born. His mother and I are both cyborgs. We didn't want our son to have fewer abilities than we do. But didn't emotion cap him."

"Emotion cap?"

"Earth Government gave us an implant that shuts off emotions. I didn't want that for my son, so that was one chip he wasn't given." He came closer and resumed his seat on the other end of the bed. "My wife didn't agree. Some cyborgs do emotion cap their children so they have the choice to feel or not. Fortunately, the decision for Deviant rested with me. My son likes you."

She decided not to ask any more questions about what cyborgs could do with their hands or why. "I like him, too."

Mavo hesitated, his expression wary.

"What? Just spit it out. Are you worried that I'm still a spy? I'm not. I really hate Earth Government and I know they screwed cyborgs over. I totally believe that. They do that to everyone. I'd never want them to find out where you are, or that so many of you are alive."

"Why would you care about cyborgs?"

"I'm as dead as you are if we're caught. Isn't that reason enough? I've already pointed out that I'm not a fan of EG or the things they do. That's the truth."

"Deviant has had a difficult life."

"I gathered that."

His gaze locked with hers. "He cares about what you think and say. You could hurt his feelings. I wanted you to be aware of that."

She let that sink in. "I never want to cause him any pain."

"I would hope not. He's risking his reputation and honor, vouching for you. He really will fight to protect you if the need arises. He broke the law to bring you onto this ship. They may punish him for it. It won't be severe, but he might lose some rank and privileges. I will make certain they take his unique situation into consideration. You're a woman who has welcomed his touch. That is a first."

"I still don't understand that."

He nodded. "We were created to be judged. First by Earthers; it was our way of life until we escaped. Some of that thinking just stuck. It's a matter of pride to produce perfection. Deviant was considered a failure. Not by me." Anger filled his voice. "Others viewed him that way. I've spent my life attempting to shield him from the worst of it but I could only do so much." His eyes narrowed. "Don't hurt my son. That's all I'm saying. You won't like the consequences."

It was a threat, pure and simple. "You love him." She could appreciate that. "I never want to hurt him. I give you my word, for what that's worth. You don't know me, but you'll learn that I'm a straight shooter. It means I don't lie."

"I hope not."

"Your son saved my life, Mavo, and I wish *he'd* been the one who'd contracted to marry me instead of that station owner."

Mavo cocked his head, staring at her intently.

She swiftly regretted admitting that. It was probably too much.

"I see."

She wondered what he was thinking but didn't ask.

* * * * *

Deviant couldn't get Venice off his mind. He ran another scan of the system, looking for any threats to their vessel. "It's clear."

Stag nodded from the captain's chair. "There has been pirate activity in the vicinity. Keep continually scanning. They've been known to use the moons to hide behind."

"Understood." Deviant pushed back his irritation. He knew his duties well. He'd been on plenty of space missions. He didn't blame the male for being cautious though. It was his first mission aboard the *Varnish*.

He scanned the area again, before addressing Stag. "May I ask you something?"

Stag turned the chair to face him. "What?"

"Why do you hold so much resentment for Earthers?"

"I was assigned to the engine room of a military battle cruiser. They treated us as if we were androids. The commander harshly punished us when anything failed. He enjoyed bringing us before the crew to make us an example of what happened when things didn't run smoothly aboard his ship. He killed some cyborgs when they didn't react to his orders fast enough, or if they pointed out when he made errors in judgment. Of course, he would have made us suffer anyway if we kept silent, after he realized he'd been wrong. It was a no-win situation. He hated cyborgs but was forced to have us on his vessel due to orders. We were the ones who paid the price."

Deviant had selfish reasons to be curious, of course. He was attempting to estimate just how angry Stag would be if he learned Venice was aboard. "Not all Earthers are bad. Some of us have joined into family units with their females."

"I'm aware." Stag tilted his head, peering at him with a look of almost suspicion. "Why are you discussing this topic?"

"It's a long shift, and we're alone right now while the rest of the crew is on break. I like to talk."

"Fair enough." Stag stood and stretched. "You were born on Garden. Earthers looked upon *us* as *you* view the machinery around you. You'd tear that console apart to fix anything that didn't work the way you expected it to, or rip out faulty circuits to replace with new ones. That's how we were treated. We were interchangeable to them. Destroy one, and just order another to take its place. It's in their nature to disregard anything they see as inferior. Add in a grandiose ego, and you have an Earther."

"The females our males have taken into family units aren't like that. They view cyborgs as equals."

"I don't believe that. Earthers *pretend* to see us as people, then use the trust they gain to cause harm."

"That can't be the case with all of them."

Stag grunted. "You were never around them. I was. Some of the crew on the battle cruiser befriended cyborgs, or seemed to. I lost three of my friends and crewmates who were lured by Earthers to sections of the vessel not monitored. They walked into traps, and were surrounded by dozens of crew and beaten to death."

Deviant stared at him. "Why would the crew do that?"

"They were bored; watching cyborgs die became a source of amusement. Some of the females flirted with us, attempting to use us as sex bots. One of my friends fell for it. Someone saw him leaving her quarters weeks into their involvement. She said he'd sexually assaulted her, rather than admit she'd been the one to seduce *him*. They made all cyborgs witness his execution.

"That lying Earther smiled at the commander and thanked him for giving her justice, and all I wanted to do was break her neck. The commander threatened to castrate every cyborg so it could never happen again. Larx was innocent. I saw that female beg him to fuck her. She pursued him every shift, but no one would believe the word of a cyborg. Barely two weeks later, she tried to lure other cyborgs, attempting to get them back to her quarters. Larx's death meant *nothing* to her, but he told me he was falling in love. It cost him his life. Earthers can't be trusted."

"Not all of them can be bad. What if you grew lonely? Would you consider finding someone to share your time with if she were an Earther?"

Stag shook his head. "No. I wouldn't trust one of them."

"I'm aware of your status on Garden. You're like me in some regards. You've been deemed unworthy to join into a family unit."

"The women don't like my attitude." Stag smirked. "I won't take their shit."

"Wouldn't that ever make you rethink your stance if you found an Earther who wished to share your bed?"

"Never. I'd have to restrain her anytime I wanted to let my guard down, otherwise she'd attempt to slit my throat. Earthers wish to kill cyborgs, Deviant. It's their nature. They are vicious and cruel. I'll acquire a sex bot if I wish to have regular intercourse. They can be programmed and trusted."

"They aren't real."

"Exactly. They feel no emotions. They do what they are designed for. I could close my eyes around one without worry that she'd attempt to kill me."

"What about joining into a family unit? Don't you wish to have a female in your life who you could produce children with?"

Stag grimaced. "The price is too high. While Earth had control over my life, the crew kept me in one of the cargo holds on that battle cruiser with some of the repair and cleaning androids. I shared everything with them. Clothing, the living space, and we worked as a unit. The last thing I want is to purposely become one of many again. Our women treat our men almost as the commander of that cruiser did. They give us orders and demand total obedience. They punish us by voiding the contract if we show any resistance. My child would become her property in that case, and I refuse to give anyone that much power over me ever again."

"But it's not that way with Earthers. I know some of our males who've joined into family units with them. They don't have to share the Earthers with other males and they aren't similar to our females. They seem docile in comparison to cyborgs."

Stag chuckled. "It's an illusion. Earthers are conniving."

"Have you ever considered that your judgment of them might be flawed or tainted by your experiences with the ones you were assigned to work for? That was a long time ago."

Stag shrugged. "Perhaps."

It wasn't much, but it gave Deviant a small hope that the male would understand if he found out about Venice being on his ship.

Then that hope was quickly dashed when Stag spoke again.

"I'd never trust one. I think all Earthers are devious and deadly. There were three hundred and seventy-two Earthers aboard that battle cruiser. Not one stood up for cyborgs or cared about the suffering we endured. You have a mother, correct?"

"I do."

"What was that like? I take it that you have a close association to her? It's difficult for me to wrap my head around family units and having a mother. I was grown inside a vat."

"We aren't what you'd perceive as close, but she has high ranking on Garden and believes my actions and words reflect upon her."

"You view her as a superior? Does she rule your life in the same way females do to the males they contract with?"

"It isn't worth the trouble it causes if I disappoint her." Deviant thought about how his mother would react when she found out about Venice, and suddenly wanted to change the subject. "I almost envy you not having a mother figure."

"I don't blame you. Cyborg women are controlling. As for your question about being lonely, I have made many friends."

"I hope you count me as one of them." He'd need the male to be forgiving if Stag discovered Venice was aboard the *Varnish* before they reached Garden.

"I do." Stag faced the front window, staring out into space. "Run scans again. I have a feeling something is off. I've had it since we left that station.

I wouldn't be surprised if someone attempted to follow us to attack the *Varnish*."

"Running scans," Deviant acknowledged, focusing on the task. He just wanted to return to his room and Venice.

Chapter Six

Venice was happy when Deviant returned to their room with food. He handed it to her then addressed his father. "Any problems?"

"None. They corrected life support without having to reset the system." Mavo inclined his head. "I must go on shift. Have a good evening." He left.

Deviant removed his boots and crossed the room, taking a seat near her. The tray of food sat between them. Venice picked up the fork and offered the first bite to him. He leaned in and opened his mouth for her, taking the meat. She tested the protein herself, liking the flavor.

"I enjoy when you feed me."

She smiled. "I'm glad. I like to do it."

"I thought about you all shift. How did you get along with my father?"

"He's worried about me hurting you in some way."

He chuckled, surprising her.

"What's funny?"

"You're so threatening."

She got his joke. "You outweigh me by over a hundred pounds and I've never been in a physical fight in my life."

"What did you do on Earth?"

"I worked at a food manufacturing plant in quality control."

"You stated they did thorough scans, to make certain you didn't steal. Is the theft of food an issue on Earth?"

"Yes. I worked where they produced vegetables and fruits." She paused. "It wasn't my job to actually grow them, but I examined the finished products before they were sealed into containers to be sold to the ones who could afford the real stuff. Android sense of smell isn't as reliable as a human's. That was my job. I was quality control, along with a handful of other people. It's always tempting to pocket a few things, since we couldn't afford to buy what was sold. We got the artificial stuff on our salaries."

He glanced down at the tray between them. "We grow our own food on Garden."

"I hope I'm not causing you financial distress. You don't have to feed me fresh stuff. I'm used to paste and cubed substances."

"All cyborgs are given access to fresh foods. Garden is nothing like Earth."

"What about the meat? That's got to cost you a lot of hours."

He smiled. "The red substance isn't meat."

"It tastes like it."

"That's queltis. It's a fleshy plant that grows on Garden. You might find this amusing since your tasks on Earth involved agriculture. We assumed it was a sentient life form at first because of its appearance. We scanned it extensively and ran tests on it, not wishing to cause it any harm. It turned out to be a plant. It tastes a bit like pork, doesn't it? It can be flavored to also taste exactly like beef. Stag, the commander of this shuttle, prefers pork though."

She took another bite, chewing it slowly and enjoying the taste. "Amazing."

"It grows quickly so we have an abundance of it on Garden. We don't hunt the animals on the planet. They are sentient. We avoid taking life whenever possible."

"I can't wait to see this place."

"I did two years of duty in our agriculture gardens in my youth. My father felt it would give me an appreciation for our planet, and it was peaceful work. I'd be happy to give you a tour."

"I'd like that."

"I'll make arrangements when we arrive home."

"Tell me about this planet. I admit I'm curious."

"I would be as well. I've never been to Earth since I was born on Garden. My father assures me it's vastly different. There's only one established city, as you would know it. The rest of the planet is lush with vegetation and a lot of ocean. The natural inhabitants of the planet are amphibian. They only dwell in the water, or the land surfaces near it in caves. We don't know that much about them since they don't seem eager to interact with us. We built our city farther inland, where they don't seem to visit often or wish to live."

"An amphibian race? That's so cool. What do they look like?"

"Humanoid with some aquatic qualities."

"You said they don't interact with you? Why not?"

"It could be a culture thing, or perhaps we frighten them. We built walls to enclose our city to avoid conflicts. Some have approached our walls in the past, but took off quickly when we tried to peacefully greet them. We're hoping in time they might wish to communicate with us and form a friendly alliance. We study them from afar and are always learning more about them. Our main goal at the moment is to show them we mean no harm, and wish to share the planet in peace with them. It takes time to establish trust."

"Your people are so not like Earth Government."

"No. We are not."

"Earth Government found a planet several years ago that could support life. It was all over the news that they'd cleansed the planet to make a new colony. That's the polite way to say they took over the planet and killed anything that stood in their way. They were actually selling animals from that planet to the wealthy who wanted unique pets." She shuddered. "But they weren't really animals. I mean, they didn't look like animals to me, regardless of what the government labeled them."

"I don't understand."

She spaced her hands about two feet apart, one over the other. "They were about this big, and I think they were the residents of that planet. They were like mini winged bird people, with two arms and legs. They looked as if they understood what was being done to them, and it was clear they were terrified. They reacted like people do, clutching at each other when they were being shown off to sell. It broke my heart. They were cute though, so

Earth Government figured they could make a profit off them. I can't imagine some asshole race coming to our planet, then grabbing people and selling them off as pets."

Deviant shared her anger. "Those poor aliens."

"Yeah. That was how I felt too, especially when it came out shortly after that they didn't survive in captivity. They probably died of broken hearts after being locked up in cages and separated from their families. I hope Earth Government never finds your planet. They'd steal your neighbors and try to make them into pets too. The rich could put them in large fish tanks or something. That's so messed up."

"We'd defend them."

She reached out and took his hand. "I believe you would. You saved me."

His features softened. "You saved me as well."

His words surprised her. "From what? You're the one who risked your life by smuggling me off the station. And even now, I know it's going to cause you a bunch of trouble if other cyborgs find out you have me inside your room."

"I was lonely. I'm not anymore. I have you."

Heat blossomed inside her chest and she knew his words had created that pleasant sensation. *Probably my heart melting*, she deduced. He could be really sweet. "I'm so glad I worked up the courage to rush inside that brothel room. I was terrified to do it."

"I regret pointing a weapon at you."

"You didn't fire it. That's all that counts now."

He reached out and ran his fingertips down the side of her arm. "I'm glad you came into that room as well. You turned one of my most humiliating moments into something life altering."

"Why were you so embarrassed? Lots of men visit automated brothels. They're very popular on Earth."

"I wasn't aware there was a shortage of women on that planet."

"There isn't."

"Men choose to live alone?"

"It's not a marriage breaker, legally, if a person pays for the use of a sex bot. A wife or husband could file for divorce if their spouse sleeps with another live person, but sex bots are considered more of a sexual aid than anything else. Bots can't result in a pregnant or expose a person to any diseases. It's a loophole a lot of couples use if they don't enjoy having sex together anymore."

He frowned. "Our males contracted into family units are forbidden to touch sex bots. The females would take offense and end the contract. It's rare to get permission from a female to use an automated brothel. I've only known one cyborg whose female allows it. He is her fifth husband, so she rarely has time to spend with him. He has high status in our society and it was probably prearranged by them before signing their contract, since he also spends a lot of time in space. For the rest of us, using sex bots usually means we couldn't obtain our own female." He dropped his hand away from her and color darkened his cheeks. "It's a source of shame to some."

It was obvious to her that he spoke of himself. "You have a real woman now," she gently reminded him.

He nodded. "And I don't have to share you with other males."

"Thank you for agreeing to my terms."

"I must be honest, Venice. I would fight any male who attempted to touch you. I like that you belong to only me. We're not contracted into a family unit but I promise you'll be the only female I touch. No loopholes, Venice. I don't want a sex bot."

In that moment, she knew she was falling in love with him. "You're the only one I want too."

He smiled. "We're in total agreement."

"We are."

"I will provide well for you. I don't want you to worry about being mistreated or what your future holds. I have mentally gone over any concerns you may have. You will be safe on Garden, and I'll keep you by my side when I travel on my next mission into space. I would never leave you for weeks alone on a foreign planet with strangers."

He glanced around his quarters. "I apologize for the lack of space we currently share. This is my first mission on the *Varnish*. It's a small ship. I am usually assigned to the *Star*. It's much larger. But my father and I volunteered when we learned the *Varnish* needed a few replacements for this mission, because some of Stag's regular crew was required to spend a month on our planet. Our council demands we stay home at least that long, for our males who work on ships. They feel it helps us keep connected as a society. I can request couple quarters on the *Star* once I legally establish that you belong to me. They will be more comfortable for you, and you'll be able to accompany me around the ship." He peered deeply into her eyes. "How are you at withstanding confinement? Please tell me the truth."

"I'm okay. I didn't leave my quarters when I traveled to that space station you found me on. It was too dangerous because there were only two women aboard. Men can get stupid, as the captain pointed out. The room was a bit bigger and I had a space port, but there wasn't really anything to see. I do wish I had access to some entertainment vids."

"I can arrange that for you."

"Cyborgs make entertainment vids?" That excited her.

"No." He looked amused. "We do not act out plays the way Earthers do to amuse others. We do, however, have an extensive library of Earth-made vids."

"Do you have any vids of Garden? I'd love to see some footage of it."

"No. We purposely scrub our computer logs of anything associated with our home planet when we are on missions. It's always possible we could be attacked and our ship taken over. Someone could discover Garden's location if we don't take precautions. We must protect our people. We store the coordinates inside our minds only. All cyborgs are prepared to fry our internal chips if we are compromised."

"What does that mean?"

He reached out and stroked her cheek. "It means we're willing to die if an enemy captures us and there is a real threat that they might acquire Garden's location. We can cause the chips inside our minds to malfunction and cause brain hemorrhages. It will damage the brain tissue around those devices so they aren't able to obtain any useful information."

"That's horrible."

"Every cyborg aboard this ship would die with honor to protect our family and friends on Garden."

"Why do you leave Garden then?"

"We patrol our space to make certain no one gets close to finding our planet. Sometimes we also need to trade for things we need, which is the reason we were on that station where you found me. Have you ever heard of Marcus Models?"

"No."

"You were held captive for years and probably didn't have access to news while you recovered from your ordeal, before leaving Earth. Marcus Models were produced. They are androids with flesh exteriors that appear human. Earth Government created them to replace us as a workforce. They probably thought they'd corrected their error by making them androids beneath flesh instead of growing them. It was another mistake. They became self-aware, too—and they believe their race is superior to all others.

"Some of those models escaped and sought out cyborgs. Some council members believed they wanted to form an alliance and were just looking for a safe haven from being hunted by Earth Government. We met with them off-planet." He paused. "They are not sentient beings, but instead, more of a single linked computer mind in many bodies. They have no emotion, no compassion, and their plan was to capture cyborgs to exchange us for more of their models being stored on Earth. We fought them and won. It made us their enemy. They are a threat to our existence *and* to anyone from Earth. Sometimes they attack space stations, murdering all aboard. We must find them before they track down Garden."

"That's terrible."

"We thought we'd destroyed all of the ones who broke free but more escaped from Earth after we met with them. Earth Government attempted to cover it up and the investigator they sent to track some of them wasn't even told the exact number of models that are unaccounted for from the storage facility where they're kept."

"They can't be that big of a threat, or why wouldn't they just attack Earth and steal more androids, if they want them so bad?"

"It's too well guarded. We've theorized that after we defeated them, they hunt for the location of our home planet to leak it to Earth Government. They'd send every battle cruiser toward Garden to exterminate us."

Venice grimaced. "Say no more. I see where this is going. It would leave Earth unprotected while they attacked you. The Markus Models would have an easier time of getting through their defenses and stealing whatever they want from the surface if the patrol battle cruisers were too far away to be of use."

"Exactly. Earth Government should destroy every model and the manufacturing plants that created them, but it's doubtful they'll do so."

"They wouldn't want to waste that much money. They'll try to fix the flaw in the first batch."

"That is our exact fear. They won't give up on the idea of having intelligent artificial life with flesh exteriors that they believe they'll be able to control. They attempted to annihilate us because we are living beings. That's not so with the Markus Models. They'll want to save the bodies and reprogram their brains."

"Damn."

"I'm sorry for alarming you. You asked why we must go on missions. That's a big part of it, aside from acquiring supplies."

"You said you grow your own food."

"We refuse to strip our planet of minerals and other resources. We'd rather trade for them or take what we need. Our city is made from vessels we salvage for building materials."

"You don't live in tree houses?"

He chuckled. "No. They are not structurally sound or long-lasting. We do enjoy our comforts, and Garden is our home. We have no interest in ever leaving it."

"Why were you at the station? Were you there to steal something?"

"We traded fresh food supplies for data chips and other upgraded equipment we need. We also were seeking information about the Markus Models. There have been no recent attacks in the area. That is good."

"It was really lucky for me that you came there."

Deviant leaned in and brushed his lips over Venice's. She returned the kiss eagerly, opening her mouth so he could explore her with his tongue.

He felt lucky as well that he'd gone to the station, and that his father had insisted upon him visiting that brothel. Venice was the best thing that had ever happened to him.

The tray between them got in the way so he just pushed it to the floor. It clattered loudly but he knew the sound wouldn't carry through to the hallway or other quarters next to him, potentially allowing Stag to learn she was onboard.

He drew Venice closer. He couldn't touch her enough. Her soft moans excited his libido. Blood rushed to his dick and his clothing in that area quickly became uncomfortable. He broke the kiss and began to strip. Venice didn't need any urging to do the same. He enjoyed watching her bare every inch of her skin.

She lay back on his bed and lifted her arms, inviting him to join her. He couldn't wait to stretch out along her side and run his hand over her belly, then lower. She spread her thighs to allow him to touch her sex. He leaned over and brushed wet kisses on her shoulder.

"That feels so good."

"I love your soft skin," he admitted. He traced the line of her pussy with his fingertips and grew more aroused when he discovered she was already wet and ready to take him inside her body. He applied a little pressure on her clit, rubbing. A louder moan came from her parted lips. "You're perfect, Venice."

"I think you are too."

He gazed into her eyes and noted no deceit. She really *did* find him attractive.

He took care to bring her pleasure, the need to please her more important than the desire to be inside her body. The bundle of nerves swelled, hardened under his fingertip, and she restlessly shifted her hips, wiggling against him.

"Yes!" She reached out, placing her hand on his chest. Her fingernails lightly raked his skin. "Deviant…"

He watched her climax then shifted his body, coming down on top of her as she recovered. He hiked one of her legs up, spread her thighs apart enough to fit his hips, and gently entered her. Her pussy tightly encased his cock and pure pleasure was found with the joining.

He rocked his hips, moving inside her, relishing the moans he drew from her lips. She belonged to him—and he was never going to let her go.

It amazed him that one female could mean so much to him, but Venice did. She made him happy, made him feel such amazing emotions and physical delight. Then he stopped thinking altogether, lost in the way their bodies fit together and the urge to spill his seed inside her.

He bent his head, buried his face against her throat, and came so hard it seemed to splinter him in two. Venice clung, wrapped around him, and he remembered to be careful not to crush her with his weight. She was smaller and fragile. He rolled a little, keeping their bodies locked together, and smiled against her skin.

He had a reason to be happy. Her name was Venice, and Deviant finally felt he had become a part of something wonderful. Her.

Chapter Seven

Venice laughed, curled up next to Deviant on the bed. The small vid player had been set up feet away, hooked to the wall beside the bed. He'd kept his word and downloaded some programs for her. She'd chosen a comedy romance since he'd wanted to experience one with her. He chuckled too.

"Earthers are silly. It amazes me that the females can be drawn to a male who acts that way. He's kind of scrawny and weak."

She ran her hand over his biceps. "Not all men are created equal. You had some help there, muscles. He's got a great sense of humor though. That's why she's attracted to him. The hunky guy in the beginning that she dated was a jerk."

"He was. He treated her poorly. She should have decked him in the mouth."

Venice grinned. "She probably wanted to avoid being sent to prison. He had high standing in society and she doesn't."

"He could have her arrested for that?"

"It's an Earth thing. It's why she fled. She was probably afraid she'd lose her temper and get payback."

Deviant reached up, pausing the vid. She turned her head, peering into his eyes.

"I'd hope you'd punch me if I ever said things that hurt your feelings. You wouldn't be arrested for it. I always want you to feel secure that you can be honest with me and not hold anything back, even anger."

That surprised her. "You're nothing like that jerk."

"Do I make you laugh enough?"

"Yes. Why do you ask?"

"No reason."

He reached up to start the vid again but she caught his hand, stopping him. "Talk to me. What are you really thinking?"

He was silent for long seconds, his gaze taking in her face. "I am contemplating if you wish I were different. I don't have a silly side the way the male does in the vid. The female in this story is falling in love with him for having that trait. You stated this was one of your favorites. That means you probably wish for a male to be more similar to him."

Another piece of her melted. He was feeling insecure. "It's one of my favorite stories because she had such a rough upbringing, and then found a man who makes her happy. She thought she'd be stuck having to marry that jerk and be miserable for the rest of her life. That's the draw. It's the fact that two people find each other and fall in love."

He entwined his fingers with hers, breaking their gazes to examine their hands. She glanced down too, noticing the size and color variations. It was a beautiful thing to her. They were different but it felt so right being together, touching.

"You're happy?"

She stared at his face but he avoided looking into her eyes. "Yes."

"Good."

"Are you?"

He met her gaze then. "Yes."

She lifted up and freed her hand from his, climbing up on his chest and peering at him. "I'm so glad you found me, Deviant. I have no regrets."

"Sometimes I catch a look on your face that reads as sadness to me. Am I wrong?"

"I can only think of one thing that makes me feel that way. Do you want me to tell you what it is?"

"Always."

"One day, you're going to tell me we're over, and that I'm free."

He appeared surprised.

"The thought hurts."

He hugged her around her middle. "Why? You should look forward to your freedom. No one wants to be property."

"I once thought that way too...but then I met *you*. I don't mind being yours. The more time we spend together, the more it isn't enough. I miss you when you're gone on shifts. I can't wait for you to walk through the door. And I get a bit depressed when I think about the day when you aren't coming home to me."

"I think about you the entire time I'm on duty."

She smiled.

He grinned back. "Let's finish watching this vid. I'm interested in seeing the end. I didn't believe I'd enjoy this, but I do."

She snuggled into him and stared up at the screen as the story finished. It was a sweet love story. It made her wish that she and Deviant would have a happy ending. There was so much uncertainty though with their future.

"You've tensed."

"Sorry."

He turned them both and pinned her under him. "What is it?"

She didn't hesitate to share her thoughts with him. "I'm worried about what's going to happen to you if Stag discovers I'm here before we reach Garden. You're going to have to smuggle me off the shuttle, the same way you got me on, aren't you?"

"We won't be docking. The *Varnish* will land on the surface of our planet. You'll walk off this shuttle at my side."

That surprised her. "So we're just hoping he's busy and won't notice me?"

"Once we reach Garden, my assignment is at an end. Stag will no longer be in command of me. He might be angry, but he can't do anything except file a complaint with the council."

"Are they as bad as Earth's ruling system?"

"No. They are fair. Twelve cyborgs sit on the council, and some members have joined into family units with Earther women."

The shocks kept coming. "Oh."

"Stag really hates Earthers but most cyborgs are more reasonable. He shared some of his past experiences with me and none were good."

"They just fear we're spies?"

"Yes. It's a valid concern."

"You'd think EG had better things to do than bother with cyborgs."

"They probably fear we want to attack Earth but that's not the case. We fled and have settled on another world. I've never met a single cyborg who wished he could return."

She touched Deviant, tracing her fingers over his chest. "I don't blame them. The only thing I'm going to miss is my sister."

"I'm sorry you had to leave her behind. It must have been very difficult."

"It was. Her husband is a fantastic man and they're planning on starting a family soon. He's worked hard to accomplish what he has with his company. I would never have asked them to uproot and start over as space refugees. Love sometimes means letting go. They're better off there. I was the one who had to leave."

"Perhaps one day you can send your sister a message to let her know you're doing well."

"It's too risky."

He leaned in and brushed his mouth over hers. "I'm glad you left Earth."

She kissed him back, feeling grateful as well. She'd always envied her sister finding her husband. Venice's luck with men had been crap until

Deviant had walked into that automated brothel. She wrapped her arms around his neck, pulling him closer. She never wanted to let him go.

A bell chimed and Deviant groaned, breaking away from her mouth. "My father has the worst timing."

She grinned, releasing him. "Cleansing unit?"

"Yes."

He climbed out of bed and she followed, making a dash for the corner, ever worried someone would pass in the corridor and catch a glimpse of her when Deviant opened the door to admit Mavo.

She stepped inside the unit, sealing it, and waited for him to tell her it was safe to come out.

Deviant had to adjust his stiff cock in his pants and snagged a shirt, putting it on as the bell chimed again. It would cover his hard-on, the material draping over his lap area. He wondered why his father had returned. Mavo should still be on shift.

He slapped his palm over the pad to unlock the door—and realized who waited on the other side a split-second before he faced Stag.

"Do you want to explain to me why we have an extra life sign on my ship?"

Deviant could tell the commander was furious. Stag had come to him, specifically, for answers, which meant he already knew Deviant was hiding someone in his quarters. "I can explain."

"Earther, right?" Stag lunged, pushed him out of the way and glared at the bed, then slowly fixed his attention on the sealed cleansing unit. "Female?"

Deviant backed up and blocked access to it. "She's not a spy."

"I knew it!" Stag curled his upper lip. "That discussion you started on your shift was your way of testing my responses. And you didn't confess to smuggling an Earther onboard my damn shuttle, so you'd already deduced I'd be furious! I've felt something was amiss ever since we left Colton Station. I should have heeded my instincts. Get her out here!"

Deviant braced his body, prepared to fight. "No. She belongs to me. The council has been notified and is aware of her presence."

"What?" Stag appeared ready to attack. "You notified *them* but not me? It's my ship!"

Another cyborg entered Deviant's room, since the door remained open. Hellion moved in between them. "Why the shouting? What's going on?"

"I'd have expected this from *you*." Stag glared at Hellion. "Were you aware there is an Earther female aboard the *Varnish*?"

Hellion shot a stunned look at Deviant, then back at Stag. "No shit? I didn't know. Where is she?"

Stag jerked his chin up. "Inside that cleansing unit. Move aside, both of you. I'm hauling her ass into the cargo bay and securing her there until we reach Garden. I'll have Kelis guard her."

"I'm not going to allow that to happen, Stag." Deviant backed up farther, placing his body against the cleansing unit. "Venice is mine. We're verbally contracted. You have no right to take her away from me."

"This is *my* ship. I can do whatever the hell I want. And you didn't ask my permission to allow an Earther onboard because you knew I'd say no!"

"Verbally contracted in what way?" Hellion glanced at Deviant again.

"She belongs to me."

Hellion's eyebrows shot up. "We're not allowed to own slaves anymore. Not even hot ones. I take it she's hot?"

"Shut up, Hellion. All that matters is she's an Earther," Stag spat. "Damn you, Deviant! Is she being tracked? Did you even check her for that? We're on our way to Garden. You could be allowing her to lead those bastards right to our planet."

"She's not a spy for Earth Government. I saved her on the station."

"You mean she set up some scam and you fell for it?" Stag spun, touched the pad, and connected to it. He faced Deviant again seconds later. "Maze is on his way. You're going to allow him to examine her. Get her out here."

"I will if you give your word to stop shouting—and you're not allowed to touch her. She'll be frightened."

Stag's eyebrows rose and he curled his lip again. "Oh, I wouldn't want *that*. You brought a plague on my ship but let's all be aware of her feelings."

"She's not a plague." That pissed Deviant off. "Why would you call her that?"

124

"Because she might well be the reason our race is wiped out if she's been embedded with a tracker. I never should have agreed to let a born cyborg on my ship. You know *nothing* of the kind of treachery Earthers are capable of committing. Did you hear nothing I said? It's a game to them to earn our trust and get us killed!"

The medic arrived, carrying his kit. "What is the emergency?"

"Deviant brought an Earther female aboard the *Varnish*." Stag pointed at the cleansing unit. "Get her out here right now."

"Your word?" Deviant didn't budge. "You aren't to hurt or frighten her in any way."

"I'm going to kill him," Stag hissed.

Hellion stepped closer to Stag and shook his head. "Let Maze scan her before you blow your top."

"My top?" Stag seethed.

"Temper," Hellion clarified. "Calm. We all want to see the Earther female. Let's be reasonable and assess her first."

Stag backed up and leaned against the wall next to the door. "By all means. Let's not scare the Earther. Deviant, open that unit. Maze, check her over. See what kind of shit we're in. I've just ordered Mavo to change course away from Garden. I'll be damned before I lead the battle cruisers right to our home."

Deviant glanced at the three cyborgs. The medic appeared surprised but not angry. Hellion seemed neutral. Stag remained furious but at least he had moved across the room.

125

Deviant turned, overrode the lock, and stepped inside to shield Venice from the males. She smiled, obviously unaware of what had happened. The unit would have blocked all sound.

"Stag is aware of you," he whispered.

Her smile faded. She paled a little and began to tremble.

He reached out and gripped her arm. "It's going to be fine. Three cyborgs are in my quarters. One is a medic. Maze needs to scan you. I won't allow anyone to hurt you or take you away from me, Venice. Can you trust me?"

She still appeared terrified but she nodded. "Yes."

"Come," he tugged on her, backing up.

She lifted her chin and followed. He admired her courage. She showed quite a lot as he pulled her closer, watching her face when she saw the other males. Her mouth pressed into a tense line and she grabbed at him, but that was the only way she responded. He took her hand, holding it firmly with his own.

"Where do you want her, Maze?"

The medic bent, placed his case down, and removed a scanner. "She's fine there, Deviant." The male straightened, turning on his device, and then spoke directly to Venice. "My name is Maze. I'm going to scan you."

"Okay."

Venice held still as Maze began at her head, lowered the scanner over her face, throat, chest, and continued all the way down to her feet. The medic crouched on one knee, scowled, then ran the scanner over her again from her shoulders to her feet.

His mouth parted, his gaze lifting to Deviant's.

Deviant knew what the medic would say so he stated it first. He trusted Venice. "She has three artificial limbs, correct?"

Maze nodded. "Yes. There's more."

"The left shoulder blade, part of my rib cage, and I have some replacement organs," Venice volunteered. "I was in an accident on Earth. Do you want a list of all the work done on me?"

"I can see it." Maze stood, running the scanner over her face. "The fractured skull you suffered has completely healed but there is some deep scarring on one side of your face. It's not visible to the naked eye. Skin grafts?"

Venice nodded. "From burns."

Maze lowered his scanner and held Stag's gaze. "This female has suffered extensive damage."

"Any trackers embedded?"

Maze shook his head. "No." He looked back at Venice. "What happened to you?"

"I was in a road vehicle accident on Earth."

"Amazing. I've never seen work like that before. I request to take more extensive scans of your prosthetics."

Deviant shifted his body, pulling Venice behind him a little. "Not if it will cause her any pain."

"My job is to heal, not cause harm. The scans would be painless. The medical advancements are fascinating."

"So she could have a tracker in one of her limbs you can't detect?" Stag pushed away from the wall.

"No." Maze turned to face the commander. "There are no transmitters inside her."

"Are you certain?" Stag seemed determined to view Venice as a threat.

"I am certain. The female isn't a cyborg but she's still been modified by technology with her three limbs. They are harmless prosthetics. The design and function of them is more advanced than what we have. It would be beneficial if I could copy and reproduce them for our people."

That news caused Deviant to relax. "She could help our race. Is that what you're saying, Maze?"

The medic glanced back at him and gave a sharp nod. "Yes. I'd love to examine her at length and ask her questions."

"No tracking devise? No transmitter? You're one hundred percent certain?" Stag's voice lowered, his anger still present.

"One hundred percent," Maze swore.

"Hacking capability?" Stag wasn't about to discount her as a threat easily.

"The only tech inside her head is a small device that conducts signals to her artificial limbs. I'm familiar with the unit. That hasn't been upgraded from the tech we have. She wouldn't be able to remote hack our systems,

128

even by touch. Her synthetic hand is amazing but not designed for that function." Maze turned and stared down at Venice. "It doesn't quite read as human-cloned skin. The organic components are unique. What is it?"

"I'm not sure." Venice leaned against Deviant, pressing tight to his side. "It feels real."

"Amazing. If I took a small clip of skin, would it scar or heal over?"

"It would heal."

"Would you allow me to take a sample?"

"You're not taking her skin." Deviant had had enough. "Back off, Maze."

The medic did as asked and returned his scanner to his case. "A tiny clipping is all I'd require. It could help our children born with skin defects." Maze rose up, gripping his equipment. "It might even help with *your* defect, once I figure out how to replicate what they grafted her with, Deviant."

"There's nothing wrong with Deviant." Venice pressed against him tighter. "I won't agree to help you if you so much as *think* about messing with any part of his body! That's the deal if you want samples of my skin."

Deviant couldn't help but smile. Venice was defending him, her fear gone. His female was smart. She'd quickly figured out she held value and was using it for leverage.

"Is she similar enough to a cyborg?" Hellion shifted his stance. "That's what I want to know. Do you believe the council will consider placing her in that status?"

Maze shook his head. "She was born to parents and her DNA wasn't enhanced. She's just had a lot of work done, but that won't qualify her as one of us."

"I want a report immediately from the both of you," Stag demanded. "How you found her." He glared at Deviant, then turned his attention to Venice. "And what happened to you, who you are, where you came from, and how you ended up on *my* ship. You go first, Deviant. Speak—and don't lie to me."

Deviant licked his lips. It was going to take hours to go over those details, and the cyborgs in the room looked as if they had no intention of leaving until they got answers. He guided Venice to the bed and both of them took a seat.

He began first. "My father demanded I visit the automated brothel." It was embarrassing to admit the reason to the crew, but necessary. He would do it for Venice.

Chapter Eight

Venice watched the cyborgs leave and blew out a relieved breath. "Stag is kind of paranoid, isn't he?"

Deviant nodded. "I apologize for the way he kept asking you to repeat parts of what happened to you."

"It's okay. I *am* a stowaway on his ship. I can see why he'd be so upset. I'm just grateful he's allowing me to stay with you and not locking me up inside the cargo hold."

"I would have gone there with you if that was the case. I'm not leaving your side, Venice."

He was so sweet, and she definitely appreciated it. "Thank you."

Deviant smiled, stroking her fingers resting in his hand. "It will be fine. I'm glad you picked up on what Maze said about your unique skin and upgraded prosthetics. The council may actually be relieved I found you. Do you mind allowing him to scan them and taking a skin sample from you? We're always trying to advance our medical knowledge. It's been more difficult since we left Earth. They have at least a hundred thousand scientists working on those things but we only have a few dozen cyborgs who took up that work. We're smart but our resources are limited."

"I don't mind. I hope anything Maze learns can help others. Do cyborgs get hurt often?"

"Occasionally. Sometimes they are born with birth defects. We're uncertain why. It makes no sense. The first generations were engineered to be perfect, yet it doesn't always get passed down to their children." He glanced at his hand, seeming to study it.

She guessed what he was thinking. "Your skin and eyes *aren't* a defect." He was beautiful to her, and she wasn't about to let him forget it. "Promise me you'll never allow some doctor to mess with either."

He inclined his head. "You're the only one who sees me as unflawed, but I'll agree. I've spent thirty-five years this way. I am unsure I'd know how to be something else."

"Good. Cyborgs are morons if they want everyone to look the same. There's a name for that."

He met her gaze and arched one eyebrow.

"Androids."

A smile touched his lips. "Ah."

"They pretty much all look the same. I used to go to the market and see them shopping for their owners. I never could afford one, but they're eerie. I won't lie. There would be at least fifty or sixty of them walking around and a lot of them wore the same clothing, factory-direct. Imagine seeing that. All the same height and size, dressed alike, same faces and wigs. They even moved alike." She grimaced. "I never *wanted* to own one. They creeped me out."

"They made cyborgs gray so we couldn't be mistaken for Earthers."

"Your size and physique would have done that. I've never seen guys who are as handsome or as in shape as any of you are."

"That actor in the vid, the bad one, was attractive and muscular."

"And had more work done on him in a surgery center, most likely. They also edit the vids to make some of those men look way better than they do in real life. I saw a celebrity once. He had a pot belly but they removed that from his vids. It's all special effects."

"I see."

"I heard people used to go to these places called gyms to get in shape, before they created surgeries that could remove any excess weight and implants that make you look as if you have muscles. It's costly though, so few can afford the upkeep as they age." She glanced at his exposed arms. "Those aren't implants."

"No. They are not."

She leaned in and surprised him with a kiss on his lips. He released her hand and she laughed as he wrapped his arms around her and easily lifted her, proving how strong he was. She straddled his lap, snuggling in close.

"I think we should celebrate," she whispered against his lips. "I know the perfect way."

"Me too."

The door chimed.

Deviant groaned, and she could totally relate as he pulled away and lifted her once more, setting her on the bed next to him.

"What do they want now?" His irritation sounded in his voice as he stood, crossed the room, and slapped his hand on the pad by the door.

The door opened and Mavo pushed past him, entering the room. "Are you both well? I couldn't leave Control. But Stag just relieved me of duty for the rest of the flight home. He's furious." Mavo ran his gaze over Venice, looking relieved. "He didn't take her from you."

"I wouldn't have allowed it." Deviant closed the door. "He was very angry."

"He still is. I didn't know what was going on. He stood up in Control and told me to take his seat, then contacted me to change course away from Garden. He just returned to Control, snapped at me about how he knew I was aware of the Earther's existence, then ordered me out of his sight for the remainder of our time on the *Varnish*."

"I'm sorry, Father."

Mavo waved a hand. "It doesn't matter."

"My actions have resulted in Stag disciplining you."

Mavo stepped close to his son, gripped both of his arms, and held his gaze. "Don't think of it that way. Do you hear me? I know you too well. I don't care about that. Stag has a reputation for being harsh with his crew. It won't affect any of my future assignments. I would consider it an honor if he writes me up for this offense. Your happiness is always my priority."

Venice really liked Deviant's father. He didn't seem upset in the least that he'd been chewed out by the menacing captain she'd met.

Deviant gripped Mavo's arms too. "Thank you, Father."

"Has Stag confined you to quarters?"

"Yes."

"I am only banned from Control. I'll take care of bringing you all of your meals. We reach Garden in the morning. Stag changed course again and

134

increased our speed. He wants the Earther off his ship as fast as possible. That's good news for us. We'll be home soon."

"He really hates me, doesn't he?" Venice said.

Deviant released his father and approached her, sitting close. "It's not personal, Venice. You've done nothing to deserve his ire."

"Stag has always had issues with Earthers. It's common knowledge." Mavo held her gaze. "He suffered major losses of the cyborgs assigned with him on an Earth battle cruiser. Some of his close friends were murdered by the crew. I was told he was one of the first batches of cyborgs produced, and saw a lot more death than most of us because of his age."

"Father had it rough as well, but he met one Earther who gave him hope that not all of them meant us harm."

Mavo smiled. "My Emily. She helped cyborgs escape, and now she's my daughter. We call her Cyan though. It's a long story."

Venice glanced at Deviant. "You didn't tell me you had a sister. Is she from an Earther mother?"

He smiled too. "It's not a biological tie. Father adopted her. She was born on Earth, with health issues, but her father was the one who created cyborgs. He built her a new body to replace her failing one. It took her a long time but she found us. She's married to Krell. He's the cyborg I spoke of, the one for whom my father petitioned the council to force my mother to birth me, in order to ensure Krell's obligation to have a child was technically met."

Venice wanted to hear more and had a lot of questions. Mavo had other ideas.

135

"May we talk alone, Deviant?" He gave an apologetic look to Venice. "This isn't about you. It's about a family matter concerning his mother."

Venice stood. "I'll go wash my face." Deviant wasn't allowed to leave and the only way to give them privacy was to enter the cleansing unit.

"That was rude, Father." Deviant didn't want Venice to think she wasn't trusted.

"That wasn't my intention. I didn't want to frighten her. She's been through enough after Stag discovered her presence aboard. Your mother will find out about the girl and cause trouble. I wanted you to be prepared for it."

"Venice isn't a girl, and Mother will have to accept her in my life."

"This is your mother we're speaking of. She is determined to find a female cyborg willing to accept you into a family unit. You agreed to allow her to make those arrangements."

"I didn't foresee Venice."

"I understand. You approved of your mother's plans because you didn't wish to be alone anymore, regardless of who she found to accept you. Now you're not alone. But your mother won't see Venice as a viable option. She's similar to Stag on her stance of Earthers."

"She allowed you to adopt Cyan."

"Cyan is revered by cyborgs. She helped us escape Earth's tyranny. For your mother to say no would have been seen as offensive by our race. And your mother aspires to one day gain a seat with the council. She evaluated my request and felt her generosity to allow the adoption would make her appear a favorable candidate to the populace."

Deviant didn't try to hide his surprise. "I didn't know she hoped to join the council."

"The female holds grudges. She only wants the position to make their lives difficult."

That hurt. His father didn't say it, but they both knew why she would hold a grudge against the council. They'd ruled against her wishes and forced her to become pregnant with a child she hadn't wanted. Deviant. "You believe she'll see Venice as a threat to her accomplishing her goal?"

"Yes."

"Some of the council members have joined into family units with Earthers. They hold no ill will toward them. She will see reason. I'll reminder her."

"Good. I just don't want her to disappoint you."

Again. They were both probably thinking it. "Thank you for the warning. I'm aware of my mother's flaws."

"I'm so sorry, Deviant."

"Her actions and words have always been her own."

"I am aware, but I still wish she had been a kinder female."

"Why did you choose her? May I ask?"

His father broke eye contact and glanced around the room.

"She chose you," Deviant guessed. "Do you know why?"

"I had earned respect for my part in our escape. At one of the Anniversary of Freedom celebrations, the council singled me out during a speech. They thanked me and shared stories of my contributions. It was a high honor, and she offered to contract with me. I agreed. I felt fortunate to be asked."

"She chose you to gain favor with the populace as well."

Mavo nodded. "The reason didn't seem important at the time. I believed she'd get to know me and learn to value my contributions to our family unit."

Deviant reached out and pressed his hand to his father's chest, knowing that had never happened. "*I* value you. You are and have always been an excellent father."

"Thank you. Are you and Venice hungry? I'll go get you food."

"That would be appreciated."

Mavo backed away and left, leaving Deviant to go to the cleansing unit, where he opened the door. Venice leaned against a wall looking bored.

"I apologize."

"Space is limited in your quarters." She smiled. "It's okay."

He offered her his hand, gently leading her out and to the bed. They sat. "I don't want you to believe I don't trust you. My father just wanted to speak to me about my mother. She's difficult, and might object to my bringing you home."

"You're a grown man. Can she do anything?"

"No." He was amused by her terminology. "I *am* an adult and have my own living quarters on Garden. It will be fine."

She released his hand and leaned in close, then reached up and cupped his face. "I'm nothing but trouble for you, am I? I'm sorry."

"Don't ever apologize. I'm glad that you came into my life. My mother rarely requires my attention. I believe my father is more worried than he should be. That's what he does. He worries about me."

"He seems like a really great father."

"He is. Don't give my mother a second thought."

Venice smiled and his mood lightened. He hadn't lied to her. His mother would probably be relieved the pressure was off her to find females willing to test him for a family unit.

"My father is bringing us food. Once he leaves, I believe we should indulge in our delayed celebration."

"I agree. I'm for any reason we can get naked."

Deviant felt warmth spread through his entire body. It was nice to finally be wanted. "You are special to me, Venice."

She leaned in and kissed him on the lips. "I feel the same way about you."

"Tell me about your parents."

Some of her happiness faded and he regretted the question. She spoke before he could tell her it was fine if she didn't answer.

"They had my sister and me late in life. Our family wasn't exactly well off. They had to bribe officials to get permission to even have children, so they saved up for a long time. They were wonderful parents." Her smile returned. "Dad was funny and my mom was very affectionate with us. They were truly and deeply in love. They were always hugging and kissing each other, as well as us. I had a great childhood."

"You speak of them in the past tense."

"They could have afforded to just have one of us when they were younger, but they wanted their children to have a sibling. Mom was forty-nine when my sister was born and almost fifty-one when she had me. Dad was ten years older than her. They didn't spend a lot of credits on medical upgrades for themselves, aside from what Mom needed to get pregnant."

She got tears in her eyes but continued to smile. "They always said that quality of life was more important than the length of it. All the credits they earned after we were born went toward our education and us having some wonderful memories together as a family. Dad died right after I turned nineteen. He suffered a fatal stroke. My mom was just heartbroken. I'd never seen any other couple as in love as they were. Her health declined within two years and she refused to allow us to take her to a medical facility. One night she went to sleep and just didn't wake up. It's like she lost the will to live once he was gone."

He pulled her into his arms. "I'm so sorry, Venice."

"They loved us." She hugged him back. "I'm glad they're together again in the afterlife."

Chapter Nine

Venice openly gawked at her surroundings as she sat in the backseat of a vehicle. Mavo drove them through a large gate that automatically opened as they approached the city. It wasn't a large one but the tall buildings impressed her nonetheless. She couldn't believe all they'd accomplished since they'd settled on the beautiful planet.

"What do you think?"

She glanced at her seatmate and grinned. "It's beautiful, Deviant."

"We take pride in everything we do," Mavo informed her from the front seat.

"I can tell. I've never seen anything like it." She admired how precise their streets were, and there wasn't any trash on the ground anywhere.

Mavo parked in front of a building and turned in his seat. "Would you like me to go up with you?"

Deviant opened the passenger door. "No. I'd like to show Venice our home on my own. Thank you, Father."

"Contact me if you have any problems. Remember we have a meeting with the council tomorrow."

"Thank them for giving us a day to settle in."

"I'll unload your bag and have it sent up to you."

Venice scooted across the seat and got out with Deviant. He took her arm and linked it with his, leading her toward the front doors of a building.

The doors automatically opened and allowed them inside. She spotted some shops on the lower floor, but it was early and they weren't open. A few cyborgs got off an elevator and openly stared at her. At least one of them smiled, so she did the same. Deviant took her into a lift and they went up alone.

"I've never upgraded my home but I could if you don't like it."

She shook her head. "I'm sure it will be great. I don't want you going into debt."

He chuckled as the elevator stopped and he maneuvered them into a hallway. Only six doors were on the floor. He stopped at the third one on the left, pressed his palm on a sensor, and it opened. He released her and motioned her to enter first.

"It's not about debt here. I was offered upgraded living many times in the past ten years but the idea of moving didn't appeal to me."

She took in the living room area first. It was tastefully furnished and larger than she expected. A full kitchen with a counter divider had been placed in one corner. The view caught her attention the most and she walked closer to the floor-to-ceiling windows. "Wow."

Deviant came up behind her and hesitantly put his arm around her waist. "I like this view. I'm high enough to see over the city walls to glimpse the ocean in the distance."

She hugged his arm and leaned back against him. "The water is so blue. And look at all those trees between it and the wall! I've never seen anything like it."

"I take it you lived in a populated city area on Earth? My father said they are full of buildings as far as the eye can see."

"You could say that. We didn't even have trees or real grass except in a few small park areas. I rarely went. The price of admission can be steep, depending on where you go. They had to put domes over the parks and vent them with oxygen so the pollutants in the air wouldn't kill the vegetation."

"I can't imagine."

"My city does have one park I visited every year for my birthday. It had flowers. We weren't allowed to touch them but the smell was heavenly, and they were so beautiful with how colorful they were."

Deviant held her tighter. "I could get you flowers. Would you like some plants for our balcony? Some cyborgs have them. It's easy to add a watering filtration system and the oxygen is clean on this planet."

She looked up at him. "I don't want you to go to all that trouble."

"It wouldn't be. I worked two years of duty in our agriculture gardens, remember? I'll take you there and you can pick out some plants you enjoy to look at. We can bring them here and give them an environment they'll thrive in. That way we won't have to tend them constantly but you can enjoy them whenever we're on Garden."

She stared out at the other buildings inside the city wall. "Where is this park?"

"You can't see it from here. Come. I'll show you our bedroom. There's a guest one too but it's empty. I've never had anyone stay with me."

He loosened his hold and she let him go, following when he walked toward a hallway. He pointed to the first open doorway and she looked in. It was a bare room and she saw that it had its own bathroom, since the door to it had been left open. They moved down the hall and entered a larger room. This one held a king-size bed, a dresser, and two nightstands. Deviant turned to her, looking uncertain.

"It's very bare. We can buy different furnishings, and I know some enjoy paintings on the walls." He advanced across the room to a big window that seemed covered by a dark film, and pushed a button. The window cleared, lightening, and revealed another view.

Venice went to stand at his side and stared out. "Oh, it's beautiful!"

There weren't any tall buildings next to them within sight, only a large stretch of land. Green and other colors of vegetation had been planted. The sight of a space vessel near the city wall wasn't something she'd expected, nor cute cottage-style house being built next to it.

"Is that a shuttle parked on the other side?"

He chuckled. "Yes. That's the *Jenny*. Coal, a cyborg, married the captain of that shuttle. Her name is Jill. She had a strong attachment to her shuttle and wanted to keep it, rather than allow us to salvage it for building materials. They lived there inside it for a while but recently began to work to create their dream home next door to it. Their androids will remain living on the shuttle once they are able to move into the house."

"They have personal androids?"

"They belong to Jill, and she's fond of them in an affectionate way. They aren't just machines to her. That section of land belongs to them, and

144

her androids grow food there. It gives them a purpose. Some of the agriculture teams are appreciative."

"Why? Do those androids help them work?"

"Yes. One of the androids, named Rune, was an advanced prototype of a sex bot."

"Oh."

He surprised her by laughing. "It's not what you might think. She refused to allow her body to be used for that purpose. She was designed to learn and evolve her own programming. One of the things she decided was that she hates to get dirty...and sex is messy."

Venice stared up at him. "What?"

He grinned. "A few cyborgs approached her for sex. She threw them on their asses and told them to stay away from her. She's a source of amusement to us. The teams enjoy watching her work her section of land because she strips naked, since she doesn't wish to get her clothing soiled. We've had a large number of single, young cyborg males volunteer to work agriculture since she arrived on Garden. She won't allow anyone to touch her but they enjoy seeing her tending to her plants, minus clothes."

Venice grinned. "That's funny."

"It is."

"Was she there when you worked agriculture?"

"No. I might have enjoyed it more if she had been. It can become boring and tedious."

A thought struck. "Is it safe for her?"

"You mean will a cyborg attack Rune?"

She nodded.

"No. She's not technically a sentient being but she's more than just a droid. She has developed a personality and who knows what she will become in time. She's continually learning and adapting. There are a few cyborgs who interact with her and study her daily. She's intriguing."

"Is she dangerous? What if someone hits on her and she kills them?"

"It won't happen. She was designed with safety protocols. She grows fruit trees, as an example, but refuses to pick them when they are mature. She sees that as killing the fruit. The other androids do the harvesting. She will defend herself but doesn't cause harm. After the first few attempts cyborgs made to seduce her, it was banned for them to try."

"And they will just follow that order?"

"Yes. We respect our laws, and Rune is unique. She's valued. No one would dare do anything to harm her progression as she develops into her full potential, whatever that may be."

Venice turned in his arms and hugged him around his waist. "I can see why you didn't move. You've got the best views from your apartment, and the space is nice."

"Do you really like it?"

"I do." She glanced around. "It's like four times the size of where I lived on Earth. My place could have fit into just your living room."

He surprised her by suddenly lowering his head and kissing her. "It feels more like a home with you here."

She released his waist and reached up, cupping his face and kissing him back. It was really sweet of him to say and it only reminded her that, once again, she wished he'd been the man she'd agreed to marry. It would have been wonderful if he'd been the real groom waiting for her on that station.

Deviant opened his mouth to her when she ran the tip of her tongue along his bottom lip. He lifted her right off her feet and carried her across the room to the bed, only putting her down when they reached it. He pulled his mouth away. "I want you."

She began to strip, hoping they wouldn't be interrupted. She already missed the time they'd had together when no one had been aware of her existence. He tore at his uniform and boots. It made her laugh as they seemed to have a contest going on who could get naked first. Venice won, and stretched out on the bed, lying on her back. She crooked her finger at him to join her and he grinned, climbing on the bed.

"We have plenty of room on this bed."

"I actually miss your bunk. It made sure we cuddled when we slept."

He pinned her under him. "I'm still going to hold you while we sleep. I enjoy having you curled up against me."

She spread her legs, making room for his hips to cradle between her thighs. "No clothes though."

He chuckled. "No clothing. You love skin-to-skin contact. I'm fond of it myself."

She slid her fingers into his hair, stroking the silky strands, and stared into the utter blueness of his eyes. "I just love touching you."

"And I love you touching me." He lowered his mouth, taking possession of hers.

They took their time, slowly exploring each other's bodies. She ran her fingernails lightly down his back, along his spine, to the curve of his butt. She opened her hands and gave his cheeks a squeeze. He groaned against her mouth and broke the kiss, trailing his mouth lower down her chin, then to her throat.

She didn't complain as he slid his body down the bed and his hot mouth and tongue trailed to her breast. He was a fast learner, something she had already discovered, since he quickly had her arching her back and clutching at his shoulders.

"I need you." She hooked her legs around his, trying to pull him up her body.

He released her breast and ran his mouth even lower. "Not yet. I love how you respond to me."

"I need you inside me."

"Patience."

"I have none," she admitted.

He placed kisses down her belly and scooted lower, using his hands to shove her legs wider apart. Venice moaned his name as he licked the inside of her thigh, inching closer to her pussy.

"I still have a lot to learn," he teased.

"I think not."

She forgot how to talk when he focused on her clit, licking and gently sucking on the bundle of nerves. His mouth was hot, his tongue lapping in long, slow strokes. His unhurried pace drove her insane and she panted, moaning as he notched up her level of need to come. She rolled her hips but he used his hold to immobilize them. Deviant was going to kill her with pleasure.

Deviant loved hearing Venice's broken cries when she climaxed. He felt pride too. He'd heard it could be very difficult to manually stimulate a female's sex drive, but no one had ever told him how stimulating it could be for the male. His dick ached from how stiff it had become, the desire to be inside her so intense it had become near painful.

He climbed up her body, hooked one of her knees over his arm, and pinned her open as he glanced down, watching as he entered her. She was wet and hot, felt amazing as he drove inside her tight confines. She grabbed at his biceps, digging her fingernails in but not enough to hurt. It felt fantastic. Everything about Venice did.

He lowered his upper body on top of her chest, smashing her breasts in the processes but remembering to brace one arm to keep most of his weight from crushing her. He loved being pressed so tight against her skin, having her under him as he rode her. Venice moaned and opened her eyes, staring into his gaze.

She belonged to him. He almost came from the knowledge that he would be the only one to ever see her beauty in the throes of passion. He loved it when she wrapped her other leg high on his waist and it gave him

149

easier access to drive himself into her pussy. Her eyes closed and she threw her head back, his name on her lips.

He moved faster, riding her harder. Her vaginal muscles clenched around his cock tighter and tighter, until he lost the ability to hold back. Ecstasy struck and he gasped her name as his seed released into her body. He kept moving though, until she came too. Then he finally stilled, their bodies locked together.

He released her leg and placed kisses on her throat when she turned her head to the side, panting. He licked at the fine sheen of sweat glistening on her skin. The slightly salty taste was pleasant. Everything about Venice intrigued him. He just couldn't get enough.

She eased her hold on his arms and caressed him. Her touch made him shiver in the best way. She bumped him with her chin as she turned her head again and he lifted up, finding her peering at him with a smile curving her lips. She licked them and he wanted to kiss her again.

"Mmmm."

"What does that mean?"

Her smile spread wider. "You. Us."

He understood. "We're exceptional together."

"We are."

He carefully rolled them over, making certain he didn't hurt her, until she lay sprawled over his body. It was his turn to run his hands down her back. Her skin was soft, smooth, and he cupped her ass, pulling her tighter against him. She felt perfect in every way. Even her weight resting on top of him seemed right.

Venice drifted to sleep as he continued to stroke her skin, lightly massaging her from shoulders to ass. He knew she hadn't slept well the evening before, after Stag had discovered her aboard the *Varnish*. He had tried to assure her that things would be fine but everything about cyborg life held uncertainty to her. Not that he could blame her for the worry.

Her life wouldn't be easy at first, living with him. The planet, the rules of their society, everything would be foreign to her. He would need to take time off from his duties to help her adjust. That wouldn't be a problem. Every cyborg who spent a lot of time off the surface on space missions was required to stay grounded for at least a month or two a year.

"You're my priority," he whispered, tucking his cheek against the top of her head. "I'll make this an easy transition for you. I don't want you to regret asking me to take you off that station and giving yourself to me."

He'd need to speak to all the vessel commanders he usually worked with. It wasn't conceivable to accept a mission unless Venice could travel with him. He refused to leave her on Garden, unprotected. Other cyborgs might approach her to test compatibility. Jealousy rose but he pushed it back. Venice had been clear she didn't want other males. He guessed Flint, Iron, and Steel wouldn't have issue with him bringing her when he reported for duty. They were with Earthers as well, and took their females with them on missions often.

He glanced around the room, silently promising to make his home appear more Earthlike. It stood to reason that she'd feel more comfortable calling it her own with items more familiar to the living quarters she'd once occupied. There was a warehouse of stored items they'd retrieved off Earth vessels. He'd get permission to take her there and chose whatever she desired.

He made mental lists of items she'd need. He enjoyed her wearing his clothing but she would need to be measured and fitted for her own wardrobe. He'd also have to discover what kinds of foods she enjoyed, so he could stock his home with them. Shoes would be needed. The one pair she'd worn when they met wouldn't last long.

He carefully shifted her off him, laying her on her side. She didn't wake. He climbed out of bed and put on pants, striding to his living room. He had a lot of calls to place. The first was to the cyborg he contacted when he needed new outfits. The tailor promised to come to his home in the evening. Venice would have clothing made and delivered to her within twenty-four hours.

He reached out to his father next, using the coms to do a visual connection. His father appeared on screen in seconds, concern on his features.

"Is something wrong? Has your mother contacted you already?"

"No. Everything is fine. I need your advice."

"What is it?"

"What does Cyan enjoy eating? Are you aware of her preferences? She lived on Earth."

Mavo smiled. "You could contact your sister and ask her."

"Krell still doesn't welcome my contacting her. He hasn't forgiven me for helping you attempt to take her from him. He forgives *you* because of your fatherly feelings, but he suspected I had other interests in her."

152

"He does show a high rate of possessiveness with Cyan."

"I understand why he feels that way."

"Take Venice to the food center and allow her to choose what appeals to her."

"I don't want to subject her to open scrutiny just yet."

Mavo nodded. "Ah. Yes. Many will stare because she'll be a curiosity."

"Exactly. I want her to feel welcome on Garden. I don't believe she realizes just how few Earthers live here. It might make her uncomfortable. I also wanted to ask you if you believe it would be a good idea to introduce her to other Earthers who are joined in family units with cyborgs."

"This is her first day here. Don't rush things. She will appreciate meeting those females in time, but give it a few days. I'll com Cyan, make a list, and go to the food center for you on her recommendations. I'll be there in about an hour."

"Thank you."

"You shouldn't leave her alone. And upgrade your security."

"You think other males will hear of Venice and try to make contact?"

Mavo leaned closer to the screen. "It's possible. She's an attractive female and not all will care that she's from Earth. They won't consider your claim of ownership since it's technically against our laws. Some might even view it as a rescue attempt to take her from you."

That angered Deviant. "It's not that way."

"We know that, and so does she, but look what we did with Cyan. We attempted to take her from Krell. We didn't understand that they had bonded. Others might make the same mistake. Upgrade your security."

"I'm on it."

"And Deviant?"

He peered at his father. "Yes?"

"I know I'm approved to enter your home...but is your mother?"

He nodded.

"Change that." Mavo cut the coms.

Deviant stared at the blank screen and sighed. His father had a point. His mother could be unpleasant, and he didn't want Venice exposed to her. He walked over to his door, pressed his palm to the sensor, and worked in more safety protocols, stripping the permission to bypass the locks from everyone except his father.

He finished and turned away, wanting to return to his bed and Venice. His father wouldn't disturb them when he dropped off the food he picked up.

He'd made it only halfway across the room when the com beeped. He spun, walked to it, and activated the screen.

Maze stared back at him. "I am sorry to disturb you."

"What do you want?"

"I wished to discuss Venice with you."

"What about her?"

"I'd like to do those scans on her limbs and take a skin sample."

"Not today. She's exhausted."

"Stag has ordered me back to duty tomorrow at noon. The *Varnish* is leaving the surface again."

"Let me know when you return. We'll set up a time."

"It's not necessary that I personally run the advanced scans. Will you take her to our medical facility soon? I shared what I had with our scientists and they are eager to reproduce the technology."

"I'll contact them tomorrow, after I talk to Venice to make certain she doesn't wish for more time."

"Thank you."

"Good luck on your mission."

Maze grimly nodded. "It may be my last. The Markus Models have been sighted. We have to get close enough to deploy the trackers in hopes of attaching to their shuttles. But they could attack us if we get too close."

"Why not send the *Bridden*? It has the ability to shield."

"They are on another mission and too far out to be of use. We are going to visit a station in their projected path and set out the trackers, in hopes they will attach to their hulls. We should be out of range before they arrive."

It was a dangerous mission' one Deviant normally would have volunteered for. It was paramount that they found a way to monitor the Markus Models' movements and figure out an effective place to strike, removing the threat forever.

"Be careful."

"Always." Maze ended the com.

Deviant turned but another message came in. He faced the coms and read the text. He'd been formally ordered before the council first thing in the morning.

It wasn't a surprise since they'd already agreed to a meeting. But the tone of it, the fact that they'd changed the hour to an earlier one, and the demand that he not bring Venice with him implied trouble.

"Damn."

He responded, agreeing to the new time and terms. He reentered the bedroom and watched Venice sleep. He hadn't planned to take her out anywhere today but things had changed. He climbed on the bed, lay on his side, and faced her.

"Venice?"

She opened her eyes and glanced down his body. "You have on pants. Why?"

"The council might be upset after all."

"Are you in trouble?"

"It's uncertain. Stag may have had words with them." He brushed her hair off her face. "I would like your help."

"Anything. Just name it."

"We need to visit our medical facility."

All traces of sleep vanished from her alert gaze and she surprised him by smiling. "Those scans of my prosthetics are worth a lot, aren't they?"

His Venice was intelligent. It was one of the things he admired about her and found endearing. "Not in monetary value, but the medical knowledge you could provide might make your staying here be seen as a necessary risk. I broke the rules by smuggling you onboard Stag's shuttle, but you could help our people. I'm hoping it will offset any anger they may feel toward my actions."

She sat up and scooted down the bed. "Let's go."

He smiled. His Venice was amazing.

Chapter Ten

Venice liked the two cyborgs who had taken charge of her once they'd entered a building a few down from where Deviant lived. She'd been intimidated by the large table they had her lay flat on, especially when another section of flat screen lowered from the ceiling, hovering just inches over her. They'd promised her it wouldn't hurt, nor take long. They'd seemed happy to see her and voiced their gratitude that she'd agreed to come.

A hand stroked her hair and she turned her head, finding Deviant crouched down next to her. "I'm right here. Are you feeling claustrophobic?"

"I'm okay."

Frax bent down, too, peering at her from next to Deviant. "We're about to begin the scans. You'll hear a faint hum. I apologize that smaller scanners won't give us as much detailed information. This might take five or six minutes in total to map all three of your limbs."

"I understand."

"We'll be able to copy your prosthetics to exact specifications. Please let us know by saying my name if you become uncomfortable. We can take a break if you need to sit up." Frax lifted out of her view and moved away. "Hold as still as possible."

Deviant played with her hair. It helped knowing he stayed close. She felt safe and protected. They'd had her strip out of her clothes and put on a pair of panties and a half shirt. It would have made her feel uncomfortable being almost naked without Deviant there.

"We'll eat as soon as we're done here. Are you hungry?"

"A little," she admitted. "You're trying to distract me, aren't you?"

"Yes. Is it working?"

"It is. I wish I were wearing more but I know they need to do it to see the connections from my limbs to my torso."

"Are you cold? I could have them raise the room temperature."

"It's more of a matter of wearing so little around two strange men."

"Both of them are in a family unit. They won't look at you with sexual interest."

She smiled, amused by the way Deviant sometimes worded things. "Ah. That makes it all better."

"Sarcasm?"

"It's just kind of funny that you believe married men don't look at other women."

"Cyborgs don't. Not in that regard. It would be highly disrespectful to their females to show sexual interest in another one."

It was yet another reminder that they weren't quite human, if that were true.

The hum began and she held still, taking slow, deep breaths to minimize her movements. Deviant kept stroking her hair.

"Thank you for doing this for me, Venice. It will sway the council into being more forgiving."

She smiled. It wasn't as if they wanted to remove the limbs or open them up to take a peek inside. That would be asking a lot. She kept silent though, afraid her speaking might mess up their scanning techniques.

The time passed fast and they took her off the table, leading her into another room. Deviant hovered close and when she sat, he crouched next to her, holding her biological hand as Quiz opened a kit, explaining the next procedure. They were going to numb her skin on her upper arm and remove a small tissue sample. She turned her head to stare into Deviant's beautiful eyes.

"I hate that you're having to go through this." Deviant frowned.

She opened her mouth to tell him it was fine but didn't get the chance to speak.

"We won't harm her, and we're taking a small sample," Frax stated. "From the questions we asked when your female arrived, we know she should heal quickly. We'll watch the process carefully to make certain of that."

An injector pressed against her skin and it was just a cold bump, then she didn't feel anything. She glanced once, saw Quiz lift a scalpel, preparing to cut. She faced Deviant again, locking gazes with him.

"Talk to me."

He used his other hand to reach up and brush her hair away from her cheek. "You're being very brave."

"I admit I hate anything to do with medical procedures ever since I woke in that automated clinic, but at least your doctors are real people.

They aren't androids that refuse to answer my questions and just dope me out again."

"Was it painful when all this work was done on you?" Frax moved into her line of sight.

"They kept me awake when they attached the limbs. They said they needed me to move them when they were testing the nerve connections. I wasn't in any pain though."

"That would have taken hours." Frax frowned.

"It did but they allowed my sister to be in the operating room with me. She updated me on her life while I'd been away and kept me distracted during most of it. They put me to sleep for the internal work they did, and the work on my face."

"The medical technology has advanced on Earth since we left," Quiz added. "We sometimes hack into medical information on ships we find abandoned in space but most of them are more than twenty years out of date. We appreciate you being so generous by giving us access to what was done to you."

"No problem." She smiled. They really were polite.

She glanced at her arm, seeing a section of skin gone. They hadn't taken much but the sight still sickened her. She stared at Deviant again as Quiz cleaned the fresh wound, then poured water over it the way she'd instructed them to do.

Frax moved closer, watching. "Fascinating! Look at how fast it's sealing from the sides. It's fusing the skin in the same fashion that stitches would. Keep flushing it out with water. It works just the way she stated."

"The elasticity of the skin is impressive," Quiz muttered. "This is much better than the skin patches we currently create to seal wounds."

"You're pale." Deviant leaned in close. "Are you alright?"

"Yes. I'm just a bit squeamish when it comes to this stuff."

He shot a look at the medical staff. "Stop with vocal assessments. You're making her uncomfortable."

"It's okay." She forced a smile.

Deviant's mouth pressed into a grim line, and he clutched her hand a little tighter.

* * * * *

"How is she?"

Deviant took a seat on his couch, motioning for his father to do the same. "Brave; and she swears she's fine. I brought her home from the medical center and she just wanted to go to bed. She's tired. Thank you for bringing the food and for helping me put it away."

"I apologize that I was delayed."

"Is everything well?"

"Krell wished to speak to me in person when I contacted Cyan. I went to their home and then the food center."

"Did he have questions about Venice? I know it's his duty to assess threats. I hope you told him she doesn't pose one."

"No. We spoke of the Markus Models."

162

"I spoke to Maze. He said the *Varnish* is leaving Garden tomorrow on a mission regarding them. Are you going?"

"I would, but Stag has made it clear you and I are no longer welcome to join his crew."

It made Deviant feel guilt. "I apologize."

"Stop. Krell is going over options of what to do if the trackers we've created work and we're able to trail the androids' movements. He'd invited other cyborgs to join our discussion, to create a plan on how to destroy the models. It's highly probable that they've created some kind of home base they are using. We just need to find it before they discover the location of Garden."

"I hate that we're under threat."

"We all do, but we will resolve this issue. It's just a matter of time. Why did you take Venice to the medical center so soon?"

Deviant hadn't spoken to his father in hours. "The council has ordered me before them in the morning."

"We already knew that."

"They updated the time and ordered me to leave Venice in my home. I fear Stag *did* file a report against me, and might have made them a little wary of Venice."

"Shit. Everyone knows Stag, though. But I understand why you'd take her so quickly now to be scanned. You can present that information to them and explain her medical value to offset his complaints." Mavo grinned. "My smart son. I'm proud."

163

"She allowed them to take three skin samples instead of one. We had a disagreement about that."

"Why three?"

"She healed so well and so fast that they felt it wouldn't scar or injure her to take a couple more. The more tissue they have, the more it increases their odds of being able to replicate it faster. She agreed. I didn't."

"Was it painful for her? Did she lose a lot of blood?"

"No. They used local anesthetic. She doesn't bleed from her artificial limbs; instead, a pinkish fluid comes from the wounds. They wanted to test that as well. I hated seeing them studying her. She's special to me, not a medical test subject. It made me angry that she had to do this at all. She shouldn't have to prove her value to our community."

"I understand, but she wouldn't have agreed if she wasn't fine with it."

"I'm not certain that's true. She feels very obliged to me for rescuing her off that station. She knew it would help me get out of trouble. I worry that she might take that thankfulness too far and end up resenting me."

"Deviant, don't take this the wrong way, but you have a tendency to overthink everything. You always have. They didn't harm her, did they?"

"No."

"She's healed now?"

"Yes."

"Let it go."

"But—"

"Let it go," Mavo repeated. "Trust me when I say, women will tell you if they are upset or if something really bothers them. They will also show you in their actions, too."

"Venice isn't like any other females I've ever met. She's selfless."

"That's an excellent trait but she's also a survivor. We both know what she's gone through. She wouldn't agree to something unless she felt willing to do so. Have trust in her ability to make decisions, or you will insult her. That will start an argument. You don't want that."

"No, I don't."

His father stood. "I'll leave you. I bought all the foods Cyan suggested are close to Earth ones, that she believes Venice will find familiar enough. What time is the council convening? I'll be there."

"You weren't notified of the change of time?"

Mavo shook his head. "No, but I'll be there."

"Nine."

"I'll see you then."

"Thank you."

He watched his father leave, then rose, entering the bedroom. Venice lay curled on her side, sleeping. He stripped out of his clothing, curling up along her back. She snuggled against him and he studied her arm, checking for any sign of where she'd been cut. There were no marks to show what had been done to her, the synthetic flesh unmarred.

He closed his eyes, holding her.

He wasn't too concerned about the council. They wouldn't dare take Venice away from him. The scans she'd provided to medical would more than justify his taking her off the Colton Station. She was invaluable, not only to him, but for gaining medical tech they didn't have.

Chapter Eleven

The council sat behind their long curved bench across the room and watched Deviant with emotionless expressions. His father sat next to him. No one else had shown up for the meeting. He'd expected Stag to be there.

One of the members finally leaned forward. "Let's begin. Deviant, you took a human woman onto Stag's ship without permission from him or us. I think I'll spare listing the violation codes you've broken. Explain to us why you did it."

A woman to the councilmember's right stiffened. "Covel, this session was brought forth to be a formal reprimand. Stag has filed insubordination charges and Deviant has disobeyed us. Your casual demeanor isn't appropriate. This is a serious matter."

Covel turned his head. "You don't like Stag. You find him as tiring as the rest of us do, with his strong stance on leadership without compassion."

"I don't even know why we're here." Blackie drew everyone's attention. "It's a simple matter. Deviant found a woman willing to sleep with him. She's inspired our medical teams with her updated prosthetics, contributing to our race, so at the end of the day, he did us a favor by choosing her. We've been given a gift. Especially when we apply what they've learned on our people who are in need of limbs. She's not a spy for Earth Government or a security risk.

"Stag can be an ass. He's rigid too with the rules. Not necessarily a bad thing, and he was required to file charges. It wasn't an option for him not to. But I dismissed them as soon as I learned why Deviant had brought the woman onboard."

"A willing sexual partner is not an acceptable reason for the actions Deviant took." The blonde woman frowned.

"You can't be that obtuse, Lizza. All females have their choice of males. You will never be lonely or lack sexual partners. It's different for our males. Especially ones who have been viewed as imperfect in any way." Zorus leveled Deviant with a cool stare. "How many times have you been offered to join a family unit?"

"None." Deviant understood the point Zorus was trying to make.

"That still doesn't excuse his actions." Lizza shook her head. "He took risks that were not in his authority to take."

Zorus leaned forward and rested his hands on the table in front of him. "Deviant, tell Lizza how many times your sperm has been requested. I looked it up. You're not sterile."

It embarrassed him but he was required to answer. "Never."

Zorus lifted his hands, opening them wide in a "need I say more?" gesture, and dropped them back down. "Deviant was given the opportunity to gain access to a female who willingly agreed to be his. I don't see any male turning that offer down under the circumstances." Zorus met his gaze. "Are you two engaging in sex?"

Deviant hesitated to answer, not willing to discuss the more personal aspects of his relationship with Venice with the council.

"They are," his father answered instead.

"I'm content with his actions." Covel shrugged. "I see no reason to punish him."

"Nor do I," Rais agreed.

"I agree," Blackie added. "Which brings me back to my original statement. I don't know why we're here."

Other council members nodded.

Lizza was the only one who didn't seem satisfied. "That's what we take from this meeting? That our males can ignore orders and rules if they are motivated by having sex with a willing female?"

"Would *you* ask Deviant to join your family unit?" Blackie asked.

The councilwoman suddenly couldn't meet any man's gaze—and remained silent.

Zorus cleared his throat. "You're outnumbered in this vote. He was lonely and found someone to be with. That wasn't going to happen on Garden. Every woman has refused him. All's well that ends well. I vote this matter is settled. Deviant is cleared of the charges and found not guilty by reason of..." Zorus paused. "Our flawed laws. Raise your hand if you oppose my decision."

Only Lizza lifted her hand.

"It's been decided." Zorus stood and looked at Deviant. "My female would love to meet your Venice. Please forward the request. Perhaps we could have dinner together one evening soon."

Deviant let out a deep breath and relaxed. "Thank you. I would consider that an honor, Councilman Zorus."

"Session adjourned."

Deviant's father smiled. "I knew it would be fine."

"Thank you." Deviant stood, him and Mavo both leaving the council chambers fast, before Lizza could speak to them if she was displeased.

They stopped outside of the building and Deviant faced his father. "That is a relief."

"Go home to your Venice."

"I will."

But he had one more meeting to attend first...

Deviant wasn't in a mood to deal with his mother, but her assistant had been waiting for him in the lobby when he'd reached his home building, there to personally escort him to her office. He entered the room, the assistant disappearing into another part of the office. His mother waited by her desk, her body tense where she stood.

Bazelle stared at Deviant intently, a look he knew too well. His mother had piercing blue eyes that never missed much. His childhood had been full of moments where she studied him in that exact manner, sizing him up.

"What is it, Bazelle? I missed breakfast and had planned to eat." She hated to be called mother.

"I was told your duty aboard the *Varnish* wasn't ideal."

That was her polite way to she had a spy that worked closely with the council. Stag had indeed filed a complaint against him. Deviant said nothing, waiting for her to reveal whatever she'd learned.

"Something is different about you."

170

It irritated him more when she changed the subject. She was trying to catch him off guard. He hated the mental games she seemed to enjoy playing. "My hair has grown nearly an inch."

"That's not it." She strode closer and paused, examining his features. "I would tell you to cut it shorter but we've had this discussion. You refuse to hear me."

"I always listen to you." He did, but he didn't always agree with her advice.

She rounded him. He held still, allowing her the close inspection. She paused in front of him again. "You have changed. There's a confidence about you that wasn't there before."

"Thank you."

"It wasn't a compliment." She twisted her mouth into a frown. "I heard about your Earther female. It's appalling but understandable."

His spine stiffened. Pleasantries were over and the verbal attack had begun. "What do you mean by that?"

"You're lonely enough that even one of *those* would seem a welcome addition into your household. It just makes my job more difficult. You will give her to someone else."

"No." He refused to even consider it. Venice belonged to him.

"You picked her up off one of those Earth stations as if she were a stray animal in need of rescue. You must realize none of my friends considering making you an addition to their family unit will allow you to keep her? It would be offensive, and that Earther's existence in your life lowers their opinion of you. Give her to one of your friends."

Anger surged. "Don't speak of Venice that way, *Mother*." He stressed the last word. "I believe it lowers *your* opinion of me, so you should just state that clearly."

A muscle in her cheek twitched. "She's beneath you. I didn't realize you were that desperate for companionship. I'll make you an appointment to test your compatibility with Dorania this evening."

"Don't." He had no interest in his mother's longtime friend, or becoming the fourth male to join her family unit.

"I realize she might not be an ideal match but she owes me a few favors."

"No." Deviant tired of her game.

Her eyes widened. "Don't tell me you've become attached to that Earther? I was told it's only been a matter of days that you've been subjected to her."

He gauged how his mother would react to hearing the truth but decided he didn't care. Warmth spread through his chest at just the thought of Venice, and he decided to be blunt. "She isn't what you'd expect."

"She's from Earth. Nothing good could come of it. I know some of the males you associate with have created family units with them, but it's an outrage! You may carry genetic flaws but that doesn't mean you have to settle for a substandard female to share your time with."

The insult infuriated him. "She's *not* substandard."

His mother advanced until she had to tilt her head to keep meeting his gaze. "You aren't considering breeding *offspring* with this Earther, are you?

It would be irresponsible and incomprehensible to burden your children with not only *your* flaws, but hers as well!"

He identified the familiar stabbing sensation inside his chest as bitterness. "Do you regret birthing me? Would you have terminated the pregnancy if you'd known the drug you took to help you conceive would affect my appearance?"

The seconds she took to answer were revealing to Deviant. He clenched his teeth, the pain an old wound.

"Those are your words," she stated calmly, backing away.

"That doesn't make them any less true. I apologize for being a disappointment." He didn't bother hiding the snide tone. "It must be so difficult for *you*."

She spun and crossed the room to her desk, taking a seat. "I don't have time for your insolence. Get rid of the Earther and be at Dorania's residence at six this evening. She'll be expecting you. I'll transmit the address."

"Don't bother. I won't go."

Her blue gaze lifted to shoot him an infuriated look. "You will make that meeting and be on your best behavior to complement our family name! Don't disgrace me, Deviant."

"You mean more than I already have by not appearing more to your liking?"

She rose up. "Don't speak to me in that tone again. My patience with you wears thin!"

"We have something in common. Don't order me to give Venice away or ask me to pretend interest in one of your friends when none is present."

"You should be appreciative Dorania would even consider you for her fourth. And stop mentioning that Earther! I am trying to forget her existence altogether. It was an embarrassment being told my son burdened our society with another one of them."

"Venice isn't a burden."

"Dorania will expect you at six sharp. Don't be late."

"Why should I have to pretend I'm grateful for joining a family unit with one of your friends when that isn't what I want? Dorania is contracted with three males already. The only gratitude I feel is because the female who shares my bed only wants *me*."

Bazelle sat down hard. "You *are* having intercourse with her. I suspected as much."

"It's more than that. Your term implies a lack of intimacy or feeling."

"I'm contacting Mavo."

"Leave my father out of this."

She ignored his demand and touched the pad on her desk. She glared at him during the silent transmission, until whatever she'd relayed ended and she shifted her hand away from the device. "He's on his way."

"Why bother? He can't talk me into making that meeting either."

"You'll do as you're ordered, Deviant! You need to assimilate into proper cyborg society at some point. That's fitting for your station in life as *my* son."

"Perhaps you shouldn't have labeled me with my name if that's what you expected."

Her expression revealed her growing anger. "I'm going to request you no longer leave Garden on those space missions. I believe the males you associate with are compromising your integrity. And I'll demand the Earther be immediately removed from your household. She is a bad influence. I'm contacting security to go there. They'll find a use for her. Perhaps she could work with the cleaning staff."

"I'm no longer a child. Don't interfere with my life." He advanced, curling his hands into fists. "I won't abide your threats. Venice stays where she is, and I'll be assigned to any duties I wish." He halted on the other side of her desk. "I would not recommend you placing your palm on that communications device and speaking her name in any context. Do you understand? Venice belongs to *me*, and neither you nor anyone else has the right to take her from my household. It would be a grave mistake for anyone who attempted it. I'd fight them with deadly force."

Her mouth parted and her eyes widened. "Deviant, do you hear your words?"

"I mean every one of them. Venice stays with me, and I don't give a fuck if you are embarrassed by that or not. You'll learn the *real* definition of shame by my actions if you continue to make your threats. I spoke to the council this morning. She belongs to me. They were fine with our verbal contract. You have no right to interfere."

"The council has already spoken to you?" She paled.

"Yes."

"They called you into chambers over your Earther already?" She reached up and touched her throat. "Why wasn't I notified? I was told it wouldn't happen until later today."

"Why would *you* be told? They wished to talk to *me* about Venice. That's her name. You need to start using it."

"Are you being disciplined in any way?"

"No."

She dropped her hand to her desk, fisting it. "I don't understand. You brought an Earther to Garden! You broke the rules by taking her off that Earther station and didn't even get permission to do it—from the council *or* Stag. That's his personal vessel!"

"The council isn't as narrow-minded as you about those from Earth. They realized why my actions were necessary. They were actually very understanding."

Her com chimed and she unclenched her fist, touching it, scanning the screen. A long minute passed then she glared up at him. "She has important medical implants?"

"That didn't take long. Your spy isn't totally accurate."

She stood quickly. "What kind of medical implants were so valuable that the council allowed you to bend the rules and let you off without any disciplinary actions?"

The door chimed and opened a second later. Deviant didn't need to turn to know his father had arrived. That was also too fast—and he suspected his father had his own spies in Bazelle's ranks. The lack of surprise in his tone confirmed it.

"You brought our son in for a meeting. Why?"

Deviant took a few steps back. "Mother and I just had a disagreement but I've made my position very clear to her."

Bazelle looked to Deviant's left. "Look what you've done, Mavo! Your son brought that Earther to Garden, and now he's refusing to be rid of her or interview with a family unit prospect. He's also sharing vulgar Earth language that he's obviously picked up from being around *her*. Talk to him."

"Is the vulgar use of language true, son?"

Deviant faced his father. "Yes."

Mavo glanced at Bazelle, his expression clearing of all emotion. "He is probably frustrated." He met Deviant's gaze again. "You knew Bazelle wished you to interview with some of her friends. Did you make it clear you no longer held an interest in doing so?"

He nodded.

His father's features softened and he addressed his wife. "He no longer wishes to join in a family unit with a cyborg female. It will only frustrate him if you're not listening to his wishes."

"There is no excuse for his disrespect."

"I see."

Deviant glanced between his parents, noticing the rising tension between them. He didn't want them to argue on his behalf. "Venice is mine, and the council agreed. You have no authority over me, Bazelle. I've made my decision. I choose to keep Venice. I never have to share her with other males, and she makes me happy. It's nice to finally be viewed as unflawed by a female."

Mavo blinked rapidly. "I'm so sorry, Deviant."

"*You* never made me feel less than perfect." He knew his father loved him and had done his best to make up for his mother's lack of caring. "You are an excellent parent."

"Mavo," Bazelle prompted, her voice stern. "Handle this."

Mavo regarded her. "Our son is happy. He wants to keep the woman from Earth instead of joining into a family unit with a cyborg female. I don't see a problem."

"What?" Bazelle gasped.

"You haven't met her. Venice is pleasant, and I viewed real emotion from her. She's fond of our son as well. They appear happy together." Mavo stepped closer to Deviant. "Our son's wellbeing is the ultimate goal we must achieve as parents, and this seems to be what he wants. I see no reason to disagree with him on the matter."

"I require your support!" Bazelle demanded. "You will talk sense into him!"

Mavo tensed further.

"Did you hear me, Mavo?" Bazelle approached and stopped directly in front of him. "That's a direct order issued to you."

Deviant watched his parents glare at each other. He cleared his throat, attempting to draw their attention. "Bazelle, don't bring him into this. He couldn't change my mind. My father has to follow your commands as a male in your family unit, but your disagreement isn't with him. *I'm* the one defying you."

Bazelle spun, shooting him a furious look. "Your father assigns your duties. You will be refused permission to take your Earther on missions. I have changed my mind. I want you off-world for long periods of time. I will not allow your perverse relationship with her to continue!"

Rage filled Deviant. "I'll refuse to leave Garden if that's the case. I'll resign my position."

Her mouth dropped open and shock paled her features. "You wouldn't dare!"

"He won't have to." Mavo spoke low. "I would never do that to you, Deviant. Venice is important to you, and I'll make certain you can keep her as your constant companion, regardless of your next assignment. I'll be sure to request family quarters on whatever ship you are sent to."

Bazelle hissed as she faced Mavo. *"You will not."*

He held her gaze. "Our son's happiness is my first priority."

"I'll terminate our contract!" she threatened.

"I knew you would." Mavo bowed his head slightly. "Do as you will."

"No other female will accept you," she snapped. "I'll make certain of it! Comply or face the consequences."

The conversation horrified Deviant. "Father, don't."

Mavo ignored him. "Do your worst, Bazelle. I would expect nothing less from you. Tarnish my reputation as an acceptable family male, but I will not sacrifice our son's contentment to please you. He has someone he values too much."

"Dad," Deviant whispered. "Don't do this. It's not necessary. I can find another position that would suit me here on Garden. I'll resign from my current duties so you're no longer involved. Don't sacrifice what you have with Bazelle for me."

Mavo reached out and clasped his shoulder. "You enjoy traveling and working with the males you've become friends with. You shouldn't have to choose between the woman you want and the life you know." He glanced at Bazelle when he released Deviant. "There isn't anything to lose. Trust me. It's a relief to be rid of her."

"How dare you!" Bazelle shoved Mavo.

"Don't touch me. You just stated you're ending our contract. I might hit you back for once."

She retreated and stared at Mavo in horror.

Mavo forced a smile, but the expression didn't reach his eyes. "You're an exceptionally unpleasant female. Did you think I'd forgotten the abuse you unleashed upon me over the years, blaming me for your difficulty in conceiving? The problem wasn't mine alone. You purposely chose not to get pregnant, and had to be forced to after you gave away the rights to my first son."

He glanced at Deviant. "I should have stripped her of any custody and raised you without her influence. You'd have had a better upbringing."

"You couldn't have taken him from me," Bazelle spat.

"It would have been easy to prove you unfit to be his mother to the council. Most females live with their children full time, but that's not what you did with our son," Mavo countered. "You only saw him when it was my turn to host you in my home, and you were too stern with Deviant. I've grown to dislike you a great deal. End the contract—or I will, Bazelle. I'd prefer to be alone than ever suffer your presence again. Remove yourself from Deviant's life as well. I'll fight you at every opportunity if you attempt to interfere with his future from this day forward."

"Get out!" She glanced between them. "Both of you!"

"With pleasure," Mavo muttered. "I'll pack your belongings from my residence and have them delivered to your current home. Who are you with this month? I stopped keeping track."

"I'll send Cluster to get my things."

"Ah. He's your favorite. I'm not surprised. Tell him to give me ten minutes. It's not as if you stay with me often or kept many possessions in my home." Mavo jerked his head toward the door. "Let's go, son."

Deviant followed, stunned by the turn of events. They didn't speak until they were enclosed inside the lift. No one shared it with them.

"Dad, I'm so sorry."

"Don't be." Mavo looked sincere. "It wasn't an ideal match. I should have ended the contract a long time ago but I stuck it out for you."

"No other female will consider adding you into their family unit once she spreads the word that you defied her."

"Sometimes it's better to be alone than with someone unworthy. I hope that's a lesson you never learn. Treat Venice well and hopefully she'll

181

treat you in kind. I envy the bond you seem to have established with her. I never had that with your mother."

"What can I do?" Deviant still felt guilt. His father had stood up for him and it had cost him, regardless of what he stated.

"Be happy. Don't allow Bazelle to retaliate in any way. You have my full support to stand up to her." He paused. "And watch your back. She's vengeful. Venice is your weakness. I wouldn't put it past Bazelle to target her."

"She threatened to send security to pick up Venice."

"Exactly. Make certain that doesn't happen. Officially notify security of Venice's statues as belonging to you, as the council agreed to. You might even want to upgrade her status in your life."

"You believe I should form a family unit with her?"

The lift stopped and the doors opened. "I would."

Deviant smiled. "I had considered it already."

They walked outside and stopped on the sidewalk. "You should have a child with her, if it's possible." Mavo smiled back. "You are the best thing I ever produced, Deviant."

"My genetic defect has a high probability of being passed on to my offspring."

His father grabbed his hand and raised it, studying his skin. He looked up and met Deviant's gaze. "This isn't a defect, in my opinion. It makes you special and unique. Be proud—as I am proud of you." He released him. "I need to go pack your mother's things before Cluster arrives. I'm sure she sent him that order before we were out of her office. We'll talk later. I'd like to get to know Venice better. I view her as family now."

"You aren't disappointed with me for choosing her above a cyborg?"

"No. You won't have to share her with anyone else or suffer loneliness. I never believed cyborgs were superior in all ways over Earthers. We're just genetically enhanced to be more physically durable. Their best qualities are their emotions and their ability to express them. I always found that attractive. Appreciate the differences and enjoy them to the fullest. You never would have received such emotions from a cyborg."

"I understand."

"I knew you would. You're my son. Go home. Venice is waiting for you."

Chapter Twelve

Deviant entered his building, his thoughts distracted by everything that happened. All he wanted was to see Venice. The lift carried him up to the right floor and he entered his home. She walked out of the hallway from the bedroom and smiled. His mood brightened at the sight of her in nothing more than one of his t-shirts. She approached, obviously happy to greet him.

"Hi! How did it go? Is everything okay? Are they going to allow me to stay with you?"

"Yes."

"Thank goodness!"

He tensed for just a second when she lunged right at him, wrapping her arms around his waist. The hug was unexpected but nice. He put his arms around her too and held her in his embrace. Her chin lifted and her smile faded.

"There's a but, isn't there? What is it?"

He didn't understand her question. Something on his face must have conveyed that.

"What's wrong?"

He masked his expression. "Nothing."

She studied him. "I don't think that's true. Is the council mad at you? Are they going to punish you somehow?"

Venice could either read him too well or she had good intuition. "The meeting went exceptionally well. I'm in no trouble and no one will ever take you from me. But I visited my mother right afterward. That's never pleasant," he admitted.

She released his waist and backed away. He let her go with regret but she latched onto his hand and tugged. "Come sit down. Talking sometimes helps."

He followed her to the couch and sat. He was in for another pleasant surprise when she straddled his lap, sitting on his thighs. Her fingers stroked his upper arms before she rested them on his shoulders. Her look became pensive as she held his gaze.

"You look sad. What's wrong? Please talk to me."

He wanted to. That was one of the many things he appreciated about Venice. She easily shared her emotions and encouraged him to do the same. "I informed her that I didn't want to meet her friends. She didn't take my decision well."

"Is she throwing a party or something?"

"She wanted me to test my compatibility with them," he reminded her.

"Oh."

He regretted sharing that information when her gaze lowered to his chest and he swore he saw a flash of pain cross her features. "Venice?"

She looked up. "That family-unit thing?"

"Yes."

She looked away from him again and tried to shift off his lap.

He gripped her hips and jerked her back into her original position. She gasped but didn't struggle. He waited until he had her full attention. "I'm no longer interested in Cyborg females."

She seemed to search his gaze for something.

"I *have* a female. You."

Tears filled her eyes but she blinked them back.

He hated that he'd somehow managed to upset her. "Do you want your freedom, Venice?" He wasn't sure what he'd do if she said yes. She technically belonged to him, here on Garden, but he didn't want to force her to remain in his home if she wished to leave.

"No."

That one-word answer allowed him to breathe regularly again. "Good. I don't want to give you up."

"You wanted to start a family. You said so. Are you willing to put that off for a while?"

He slid his hands around her to keep her in his arms. "I do want a family. You can have children, can't you?"

Her grasp on his shoulders tightened. "You want them with *me*?"

"My flaws will probably be passed to our offspring. Cyborgs are very aware of any variations in other cyborgs. Will that trouble you?"

More tears filled her eyes. "Our kids would be perfect if they looked just like you."

She always made him feel good. The tightening sensation he felt inside his chest wasn't pain, but joy. "Thank you."

"You're not flawed. You're wonderful." She leaned in closer, until her breasts pressed against his uniform. "I'd stay with you forever if you'd let me."

"I'd encourage it."

Her smile returned and he completely relaxed. His mother was wrong about Venice. She hadn't even met her. No cyborg female could ever make him feel the way this Earther did. Of course, emotions weren't something his mother approved of.

"Do you want to talk about it?"

He jerked away from his thoughts. "About what?"

"Your mom. I take it she wasn't happy that you didn't want to meet her friends?"

"She has expectations of me that I refuse to fulfill."

"She wants grandkids? Did you tell her I can have babies? I can. Maybe that will make her happy."

He didn't want to spoil her mood but he couldn't lie to her either. She was an honest individual who deserved honesty in return. "She wanted pure cyborg offspring produced by myself and a female."

"Oh."

"It's not personal. You're from Earth."

"I guess I can't blame her, considering the history with Earth Government. They did try to wipe out your entire race. I could meet her and she'd see I'm not anything like them."

"No!" He regretted the outburst when she startled. The hurt look came next. He massaged her hips. "It's not you, Venice. My mother isn't pleasant at *any* time, to anyone. She would be cruel, and I never want to subject you to that."

"I understand."

"Even I don't enjoy spending time with her," he admitted. "She has a special talent for being insulting. I never want you to suffer her, Venice. It would anger me. I've had a lifetime to adjust to her behavior but you haven't."

Her expression cleared of pain. "That must have been rough growing up."

"I want to protect you from her."

"That bad, huh?"

"Worse. My father ended his contract with her today. They are no longer joined into a family unit."

She blinked a few times, appearing surprised. "Why?"

"He stood up for my right to be with you. She demanded he take her side but he refused. He wants what is best for me. That is you."

"And that caused them to file for divorce?"

"Their contract is already broken. They are no longer a family unit. My mother would have had it recorded by the time my father got home. She ordered him to take her side. He refused. It's a breach of their contract for him to refuse her demands, and so she ended it with him."

"Oh, Deviant. I'm so sorry." Tears filled her eyes. "It sounds as if he did himself a favor though, if she's that mean. Every woman should want her children to be happy."

"My father implied the same."

"He's a wise man." She closed her eyes and tucked her head against his neck. He liked the feel of her nestled there, and the way her warm breath tickled his skin. "I wish I could make all this better for you."

She was with him, in his arms. "You do, Venice." He smiled. "Just stay right where you are."

"I can do that."

He ran his hands over her lower back and massaged her ass. "I enjoy having you this close. You make me feel alive."

"I'll stay here as long as you allow it."

"Forever then."

She chuckled. "Perfect."

He hesitated. "Venice?"

She lifted her head and peered at him. "What?"

"I'd like to join a family unit with you. It would be the equivalent of marriage. Would you agree?" He held his breath when she hesitated.

"On one condition."

"Name it."

"Promise you'll never let me go, or ask me to end our contract. I don't ever want to lose you."

It was an easy request. He never wanted to be without Venice. "I give you my word of honor. I want the same promise from you."

She released his shoulder and used a finger to make a cross over her chest. "I cross my heart."

"What does that mean?"

She grinned. "It's a promise."

"I'll make the arrangements for tomorrow. There's one more thing we must discuss."

"Okay."

"My mother is vindictive. Never answer my door. I've upgraded my security measures to only allow myself and my father entry. My computer will send me a signal if I'm not home and someone tries to visit. On the off chance that security arrives and breaches the doors before I return, state clearly that you belong to me, Venice. Refuse to go with them until I am present. It's the law, and they must follow it if you state that." He hated to instill fear in her.

Her eyes widened a little but then she nodded. "Got it. She's a real bitch, huh?"

"Yes. She's powerful but she can't violate the law. You'll be safer once we're joined into a family unit."

"Is that why you want to marry me? Just to keep me safe?"

190

"No." He smiled. "I wanted to do that before Bazelle made her threats. It just made me ask you sooner than I'd planned. I thought you might need more time to make that decision, but I'm so glad that you have agreed."

"I wanted to stay with you from the first day we spent together." Tears flooded her eyes. "I was terrified you'd want a cyborg instead of me."

"You're a thousand times better, and you make me feel so many wonderful things, Venice."

"I love you."

He pulled her close, probably holding her too tightly. "That is the best gift I've ever received, and I will cherish you. I feel the same."

Venice knew Deviant loved her. He didn't say the words yet but she hoped one day he would. The most important part was that he wanted to marry her. She snuggled tighter against him. He'd even brought up having children.

All the dreams and hopes she'd had since leaving Earth, of having a family, would come true. This time, though, it would be with the right man, one she had fallen in love with, and not some scam artist intent on luring her into sexual slavery.

The only down side seemed to be Deviant's mother. It really bothered her that she was the cause of strife between them. Would he end up regretting marrying her one day?

She lifted her head, peering into his eyes. They were so blue, so beautiful, and he meant everything to her. She'd make sure he had no regrets. It was that simple. No matter how bad his mother was, regardless of what kind of trouble the woman might cause, Venice and Deviant would weather it together.

She kissed his neck. "It's going to be fine." She said it for herself, as much as for him. "Do you know what will make us both feel better?"

He massaged her ass. "Sex?"

"Always." She pulled away, climbed off his lap, and backed up. She grinned. "You've had a stressful morning. Let's forget about everything but each other for a while."

He rose up and followed, smiling. "I enjoy how you think."

She turned, going into the bedroom and removing her clothes, and then climbed on the bed. Deviant stripped fast and she took in every beautiful inch of him. Cyborg women didn't know what they were missing out on—and she'd never been so grateful. He was all hers.

He climbed onto the end of the bed and crawled to her. She lay back, opening her arms and spreading her thighs. She'd been secretly terrified his council would try to tear them apart, or he'd be in serious trouble for saving her life. He'd refused to allow her to go with him. She knew he wanted to protect her from facing off against a group of possibly angry cyborgs.

All that worry suddenly came out as he lay down on top of her and she latched onto his mouth. Venice kissed him, putting all the fear she'd felt while he'd been gone into it. She frantically clutched at him, pulling him even closer. He tried to slide down her body but she wrapped her arms around his neck. She wasn't in the mood for foreplay. She just wanted

Deviant inside her. There was a desperation to her actions but she didn't care. She could have lost him, and wasn't about to forget it anytime soon.

Venice spread her legs wider and wrapped them around his waist, rolling her hips.

He tore his mouth away and lifted his head, staring into her eyes. "What's wrong?"

"I just want you now."

He cupped her cheek. "You were frightened. No one is ever going to separate us, Venice. I won't allow it to happen."

"Good. I'm counting on that. I'd be devastated. I've been in love with you since the first day we spent together. Make love to me now. Please? I need you inside me."

He reached between them, using his fingers to play with her clit. Venice moaned, rubbing her pussy against his hand. She was so wet, and he almost brought her to climax before withdrawing his hand and shifted his body above hers, nudging her with his cock. She wrapped her legs tighter around him as he eased inside, filling her, connecting their bodies.

"Yes..."

"I love you, Venice," he rasped.

She held his gaze as he began to slowly move, fucking her. It felt so good she fought to keep her eyes open. She clung to his shoulders, rocking her hips to match his thrusts. He was incredibly hard, thick, and it felt too good to hold off for long.

She threw her head back, crying out his name. He came right after she did, burying his face against her throat.

They lay entwined on the bed, Deviant keeping her pinned under him.

She wasn't going to lose him. He wanted to marry her. Tears filled her eyes but she blinked them back. It was a relief not to worry about him walking away from her one day.

Chapter Thirteen

Venice stared in the bathroom mirror and smiled. The dress Deviant had bought for her to wear for their ceremony looked perfect. It was a summery cut with short sleeves, revealed a little cleavage, and flowed to just below her knees after gathering a little at the waist.

She heard a fast knock, then the bedroom door opened.

"Venice?"

She exited the bathroom and smiled at Mavo. "Hi."

"My son wanted to escort you to the ceremony, but I told him it's an old Earth tradition not to see the bride before a wedding. Are you ready to leave?"

She nodded. "How do I look?" She turned in a slow circle. "The clothing guy came to fit me and delivered this a few hours ago."

"You're beautiful. I'm glad you're wearing your hair down."

"Deviant loves it that way. I put it up this morning to show him different styles but this is the one he chose."

"He was correct. Are you ready to go?"

"I am."

"Are you nervous?"

"No." She wasn't. "I'm excited."

"Deviant chose a beautiful spot for you to bind your lives together."

"Where is it?"

Mavo grinned. "It's a surprise. Let's go. *You* may not be nervous but my son seemed terrified you'd change your mind."

"I love him. I can't wait to get married."

"He asked for an Earth ceremony to bind you in marriage. There's a contract to sign but it will be quick."

She was touched. Deviant really made her feel special. "Let's go. I'm so ready."

He led her into the living room and picked up bound flowers off the table, holding them out to her. They were white and beautiful, almost looking like roses. "My gift to you. They are edible too."

They were too pretty to eat. She didn't mention that aloud. "Thank you!"

"I welcome you to our family, Venice." He offered his arm. "I read up on Earth ceremonies. I would be honored to give you away in place of your father."

She fought hard not to cry, emotional at the reminder of her father. "That's so sweet. I'd appreciate that so much."

He grinned and led her out of the home, to the lift, and down to the lobby. Instead of taking her out of the front of the building to the street, they exited out a back door and entered the agriculture area she had seen from the bedroom window.

Mavo lifted his hand and curled it over hers, resting on his arm. "We're almost there."

"I hear water."

"There's a stream ahead."

"I saw it from the windows."

She spotted a bridge over the stream and Deviant stood there, along with two other men and a woman with waist-long black hair. "Who are the people with him?"

"The one with scars is Krell, my best friend. The female is Cyan, my adopted daughter and Krell's wife. She just had their son but found a babysitter. She feared their child might cry and disturb your ceremony. The other male is Zorus. He's a council member who will perform the marriage. Please don't stare at Krell's scars. I know he has many of them."

"I won't." She wished the couple had brought their baby. She'd love to see him. Part of her wondered, too, if the child had ended up with his father's coloring or his mother's. It didn't matter but it was a curiosity.

She focused on Deviant as he turned to stare at her, watching her approach. He had put on a tight black uniform that outlined his gorgeous body. Her heart pounded and she smiled at him. She had to be the luckiest woman ever. He smiled back at her.

Mavo led her to the center of the bridge, where everyone waited. She could easily tell who was who once she glanced at the men. Krell's scars were noticeable but she just nodded at him, avoiding staring. The other man had to be Zorus, the council member. He looked nice enough as he inclined his head her way.

"You are so beautiful!" Deviant blurted.

She felt heat creep into her cheeks as she stared at him again. "You take my breath away too."

"I already love her," the woman stated.

Venice studied Cyan. "Hello."

"We'll be the best of friends." Cyan winked. "Welcome to the family. Now marry my brother before he becomes crazier than he already is. He's been pacing, waiting for you, and I've had to stop him twice from rushing home to make sure you were going to show up."

Venice gazed lovingly at Deviant. "I wouldn't miss marrying you for anything."

Zorus cleared his throat. "Let's begin. I apologize for the rush, but it's going to be hot today." He smiled. "And I remember my wedding day. I just wanted everyone to leave so I could get Charlie alone and naked in our bed. I know you, Deviant. I'm certain you feel the same way about your bride."

Venice blushed a little but was amused. "I'm all for that."

"I will stand in as her father," Mavo announced.

Zorus moved between them. "It is my pleasure to bring this couple together in matrimony today. Mavo, please escort the female to your son."

He led Venice forward a few feet to stand in front of Deviant and released her, backing away. "With pleasure."

Deviant took her flowers, passing them to Cyan, then clasped both of her hands in his. "You honor me, Venice."

"I'm the lucky one," she whispered back.

Zorus began. "Do you, Deviant, take Venice to be your wife? Do you promise to love and cherish her? Do you swear to protect her from all harm and see to her every need to keep her happy and content?"

"I do," Deviant rasped.

"Venice, do you take Deviant to be your husband? Do you promise to love and cherish him? Will you allow him to protect you from all harm and attempt to make him happy and content?"

"I do." The vows weren't quite what she expected but she liked them.

"Deviant has asked for one more vow to be added that you both take." Zorus paused. "Do you both agree this shall be a lifelong commitment to each other, that you shall never request this contract to be dissolved?"

"I swear," Deviant stated, loud and clear.

"I do too." It was so sweet that he'd remembered, and that he never wanted to lose her, either. "Forever."

Deviant squeezed her hands, his grin widening. "Forever," he repeated.

Zorus reached inside the pocket of the gray outfit he wore and removed a box. "The rings."

Deviant released Venice and accepted the box. He opened it and showed her two matching rings. "I hope you don't mind. Some cyborgs get tattooed but I would never want to cause you any pain or mar your skin. I wanted to honor Earth traditions."

She nodded, touched. "I'm so glad." They were made out of some shiny, bright blue material that reminded her of Deviant's eye color, just simple bands, but silver had been added to them to make a strange yet beautiful design.

"They are our names in the cyborg language." Deviant took out each ring and his father accepted the box. "They were made from an ocean stone found here on Garden." He cleared his throat. "You said you love my eyes, and they nearly match the color of them."

"I love them." And she loved him even more for being so thoughtful and wonderful.

Venice lifted her left hand and Deviant gently placed the ring on her finger. He handed her his and she did the same, pushing it onto his finger.

He clasped her hands again and looked at Zorus. "Seal the contract."

"It is my official honor to declare—"

"Wait!" a female voice called out. "Halt this immediately!"

Venice twisted her head, stunned, as a lovely gray woman with black hair quickly approached. She wore a red dress with matching boots—and four cyborg men followed her.

"Damn it," Mavo hissed and moved fast, crossing the bridge to intercept them. "Don't do this, Bazelle. This is our son's wedding."

"Get out of my way!"

Venice almost winced at how strongly Deviant's hold on her hands became. She instantly didn't like his mother. She was a beautiful woman, but she was also trying to ruin their wedding.

Mavo didn't budge, blocking them from stepping onto the bridge. "Leave *now*. You were not invited."

Bazelle tried to sidestep around Mavo but he moved with her. She shoved at him. "I'm more than aware. I demand to speak to that Earther.

200

Councilman Zorus, I believe this female has been given false information and is about to enter a contract she doesn't understand."

Venice turned fully toward her, barely managing to keep her mouth from falling open. Deviant's mother made it sound as though she was trying to protect Venice from something—and she wasn't buying that for a second. "I love your son. I am marrying him because I want to. There's nothing false about how I feel."

"What are you attempting to do, Bazelle?" Zorus didn't sound happy. "You heard Venice. She wishes to enter a family unit with Deviant. Leave."

"Don't do this, *Mother*." Deviant nearly snarled the word.

"Does she know that she could choose any other cyborg on this planet who has better standing? Earther!" Bazelle yelled. "Did Deviant inform you that you have the right to join with many males in a family unit? Ones with higher standing on Garden? Did he make you aware that his flaws have a high probability to be passed down to any offspring you may have with him, and other children will shun *yours*?"

Venice opened her mouth but Bazelle wasn't done.

"I brought four single males with me. They are handsome, with stronger status in our society. They have no flaws. You wouldn't be stuck with just one of them when you grow bored of their company. On Garden, you choose who you live with, and for how long. I believe my son hasn't informed you of how our society works, and is purposely keeping you in the dark. Councilman Zorus, I demand we take this before the council so they may question that Earther about how much she knows before you seal their contract! She is completely unaware."

Venice wiggled her hands and slipped them out of Deviant's. He let her go, and she took a few steps closer to the tall cyborg woman. "Oh, I'm *aware* alright. You're such an unfit mother! Wow. You're not here on my behalf. You're pissed because your son isn't doing what you ordered him to do, and you're being petty and vindictive. I may have been raised on Earth, but I also know what a bitch is. That would be *you*. I know I'm allowed more than one cyborg husband, but guess what? I only want Deviant. And don't you dare call *anything* about Deviant flawed. Look in a mirror, lady. There's something seriously wrong with you. Maybe when you were created they forgot to put a heart in your chest."

Bazelle's face darkened an ugly shade of gray. "My relationship with Deviant is none of your business!"

"Right back at you. You weren't invited to our wedding. Now I totally understand why. Do you know what the saddest part is? Deviant rescued me from certain death, has shown me nothing but love and compassion, and you're too stupid to see how amazing he is."

The cyborg woman smirked. "So you admit it's only gratitude that made you accept a contract with him."

"Don't twist my words. I feel gratitude, but I also love him. I am *in* love with him. I bet you've never known that emotion, have you? Deviant is funny and sweet, intelligent and loving. He sure didn't inherit any of those traits from *you*. Get lost—and take your men with you. The only man I want is right behind me."

She turned, staring up at Deviant. "Let's ignore her." She glanced at Zorus. "Can we get on with this?"

202

"No," Bazelle shouted. "I'm protesting this contract!"

"Denied," Zorus announced. "Leave, Bazelle. Otherwise, I'll have charges brought against you for disturbing the peace."

"You wouldn't dare!"

Zorus snorted. "I would love to. Push me, Bazelle. I've never been a supporter of yours. I don't like the way you look at my Charlie at social events, as if it's an insult to have her amongst our company."

"You admit this is personal then." Bazelle took on a haughty tone. "Recuse yourself immediately and convene this matter before the council!"

"That's not going to happen. You're a known purist. It's laughable that you'd use the excuse of coming to the aid of Deviant's female. You gave your son orders and he defied you. Accept it. Do you never grow tired of playing these stupid manipulation games? I'm having none of it."

Zorus turned his attention back to them. "As I was saying, it's my official honor to declare that Deviant and Venice have joined in an unbreakable family unit of two." He reached inside his shirt, pulling out a small pad. "Place your hand on this to seal the contract."

There was a scuffle behind Venice, someone gasped, but she didn't bother looking. Instead she put her hand on the pad. It flashed as it scanned her palm. Deviant moved her hand and placed his on the scanner.

Venice took that moment to glance back, a bit stunned to see that Bazelle was being held by Mavo. At first glance, it almost looked loving, his arm around her waist, his face bent next to hers as he whispered in her ear, and his other arm wrapped around her upper body.

Then she noticed Bazelle was off her feet by a few inches and she tried to kick Mavo in the shin. He shifted his leg, avoiding the blow. Her mouth opened but Mavo was faster, releasing her upper body and slapping his palm over her lips.

Venice stared up at Deviant, gauging his reaction to his parents. He peered over her head, a muscle in his jaw tensed, but then he smiled down at her.

"It's done and recorded," Zorus stated loudly. "You can let her go, Mavo."

Venice watched as Mavo dropped the woman on her feet and gave her a gentle shove, backing away.

"You bastard!"

"I've been called worse by you."

Bazelle took a wild swing at Mavo but he ducked, avoiding it, and backed up farther, snarling at her. "You attempt that again and I *will* hit you."

His ex fumed and glared at the four men she'd brought with her. "Do something!"

They turned around and walked down the path, leaving.

Bazelle glared at Mavo. "I'll make you pay for this!"

"No, you won't." Zorus walked down the bridge. He gripped her arm, forcibly pulling her along the path with him. "You want to talk to the council? I am in communication with them right now. We'll discuss your threats, the way you disturbed the ceremony, and attempted to stop a couple from joining into a family unit—which you don't have the right to do as a female. Only males can challenge."

She hissed something at him but they were too far away for Venice to hear.

Mavo turned, looking grim. "I'm sorry."

Deviant put his arm around Venice from behind. "So am I."

"That was a memorable wedding." Venice took a deep breath and lifted her chin, twisting her head to look at him. "Do you know what counts the most?"

Deviant held her gaze. "What?"

"We're married. And there's one more Earth tradition I insist upon."

"What's that?"

She turned in his arms, reached up, and placed her hands on his shoulders. "You're supposed to kiss the bride."

He grinned. "I would love to."

Venice went up on her tiptoes and closed her eyes, loving the feel of Deviant's lips against hers. They were married, despite his mother trying to bust up their wedding. He was hers and she was his. That was all that mattered.

The kiss ended too quickly and she opened her eyes. It hurt her to see the sadness in his gaze.

"I apologize for her actions."

"We knew she was going to try something, right? Guess what? She doesn't scare me, Deviant. She wasn't able to stop us from binding our lives together. I think I made it very clear to her that I don't like her and I'm not stupid enough to fall for her crap."

Amusement sparked in his bright blue eyes. "I saw and heard."

"Sorry about that. She pissed me off. I can have a temper at times. But you did say to never be afraid to let it rip when I got angry."

The way Venice worded things had Deviant chuckling. "Yes, I did. Never apologize for standing up for me. I appreciate everything you said to her."

"I meant every word. I'm so lucky you're mine."

Deviant felt *he* was the fortunate one. "I feel the same. Let's go home."

She snuggled against him tighter. "I love the sound of that."

"I have a few surprises for you tomorrow."

"I can't wait to find out what they are."

He had talked to a few friends and made arrangements to take Venice to see all the Earth things stored on Garden. She could make their home more Earthlike and comforting. He also planned to take her on an extended tour of the agriculture area. She did seem to love flowers and plants.

"I just want you to be happy," he stated honestly.

"I am."

Chapter Fourteen

A few days later

Nerves had Venice pacing between the kitchen and living room, her gaze darting to the door. Deviant said he'd be home at six but was running a little late. She glanced at the clock, seeing it had only been five minutes, but she worried. His mother hadn't tried anything else since their wedding but she knew that could change.

The door finally opened and she grinned, taking in her handsome husband. He wore light blue that day, the snug uniform showing off every glorious detail of his fit, muscular body. She figured she'd never stop appreciating the sight.

He closed the door and met her gaze from five feet away, where he'd paused. Something was behind his back and the grin on his face told her he'd brought her another surprise. He loved to give her gifts. "I missed you."

"I missed you too." She rushed at him but he stepped back, bumping the door. She froze. "What is it?"

His grin widened. "Close your eyes."

"You're spoiling me." She did it though, squeezing her eyelids together. "Not that I'm complaining."

"You deserve it. You're the best wife a male could possibly have."

He always knew the right thing to say, too. She heard him move around her and one of his arms encircled her waist, drawing her up against him. He leaned in a little, his warm breath fanning against her ear.

"I so enjoy coming home to you."

"I hate it when you leave," she admitted. "I missed you, even though you were only gone a few hours. How is your father?"

"He's well. He leaves on the *Star* tonight. You could have come with me to say goodbye to him."

"I thought you two might need some quality time together alone. How is he doing since the divorce?"

"Dissolution of contract," he corrected, brushing a kiss on the shell of her ear. "He seems relieved. They weren't happy."

"Can I open my eyes now?"

His other arm brushed hers. "Yes."

She did, staring at his closed fist in front of her. He opened his palm, revealing a data disk. "What's on it?"

"I spoke to Flint. He happened to have a lot of Earth entertainment vids and gave me copies of his wife's favorite ones. She highly recommended these for us. They are supposed to be romantic, with humor in them. I thought we could curl up together and watch them over the next few weeks that I've taken off."

She stared up at him. "Are you sure you don't want us to go on this mission with your dad? I know you normally travel together."

"A freighter was reported abandoned three sectors out and they are going to investigate, then haul it to Garden if any parts of it can be salvaged. They've estimated it will take two weeks. It should be easy for them, and I'd much rather spend this time with just you. It's our honeymoon."

"You really have brushed up on Earth traditions, haven't you?"

"Yes. We are going to relax, watch vids, and enjoy being together."

She turned in his embrace, wrapping her arms around his neck. "It sounds perfect."

"It does."

"I think we're overdressed. Dinner is almost ready. I cooked."

He inhaled, smelling something good. "You didn't have to."

"I wanted to. Have you ever eaten in bed?"

"We ate meals seated on my bunk on the *Varnish*."

She laughed. "Not the same. You're in for a treat. Go get naked, set up a vid in there, and I'll bring in our food in a few minutes. We'll have dinner and entertainment. I just have to take it out and put it on plates."

"That sounds like fun."

She let him go and backed away. "It does. I'm going to feed you."

"You spoil me."

"Just wait until after we've finished eating and the vid ends. I have an ulterior motive. I'm going to make you work off that meal." She winked. "I really missed you. I was thinking about new sex positions we haven't tried yet."

"I can't wait." He clenched the data disk and headed toward the bedroom, but then paused, turning around. "I have one more surprise for you."

"What is it?"

"My father is going to pass a lot of satellites on his assignment."

"I don't know what that means?"

He approached her, stopping feet away. "He can send a message to Earth that won't be traceable. We discussed it. I know it bothers you that your sister doesn't know where you are, but I thought you could send her a message to let her know you're happy."

Tears welled in her eyes. "I'd love to do that, but it's too dangerous. I mean, if EG ever figured out she helped me escape from—"

He placed a finger on her lips, silencing her. "My father and I discussed this at length. Your sister and her husband own a business making shuttle parts. You could send a coded message that only she would understand. Something along the lines that the parts you received have worked out extremely well and you are happy. That way, she would know you're alive and well." He moved his finger off her mouth, cupping her cheek. "It would give you both peace."

"I love you so much, Deviant. Thank you. I can think of something that would work."

"I knew you could. I'll transmit it to my father and he'll send your message on once he finds a safe location to do so. I love you more than words can say, Venice. You saved me from a life of sorrow and loneliness. Thank you for coming into that room."

"You saved me too."

"We saved each other. You were so brave to approach me."

"All I did was work up the nerve to seduce the sexiest man I've ever seen."

"I will be eternally grateful."

"Me too."

He kissed her, a light brush of his lips over hers. "Get the food. I'll set up the vid. I want to make love to you after we eat."

She smiled.

He grinned back. Venice was the best thing that had ever happened to him. She made him happy...and he would spend the rest of his life making her happy, too.

Printed in Poland
by Amazon Fulfillment
Poland Sp. z o.o., Wrocław